"Excuse me,"

The man's voice interrupted Olinda's thoughts.

"You appear to be sitting at my table," he continued.

"Your table?" Olinda challenged.

"That's right. This is my table. Not that I have any objection to sharing it. The company of a young, attractive woman is not something I am ever particularly eager to deny myself."

So he hadn't changed. The playboy head of De Chevalley Foundation, renowned for its work in the area of scientific research, was still the shameless womanizer of before! A man who broke hearts without a moment's hesitation, who treated females as a form of cheap entertainment; a man without any moral scruples whatsoever.

The very last thing Olinda wanted was Guy de Chevalley sitting at her table, and she intended to make her wishes known.

Stephanie Howard is a British author whose two ambitions since childhood were to see the world and to write. Her first venture into the world was a four-year stay in Italy, learning the language and supporting herself by writing short stories. Then her sensible side brought her back to London to read Social Administrations at the London School of Economics. She has held various editorial posts at magazines such as *Reader's Digest, Vanity Fair,* and *Women's Own,* as well as writing freelance for *Cosmopolitan, Good Housekeeping* and *The Observer.* She recently spent six years happily trotting around the globe, although she has now returned to the U.K. to write romance novels.

Books by Stephanie Howard

WICKED DECEIVER

Stephanie Howard

Harlequin Books

TORONTO • NEW YORK • LONDON
AMSTERDAM • PARIS • SYDNEY • HAMBURG
STOCKHOLM • ATHENS • TOKYO • MILAN

Original hardcover edition published in 1990
by Mills & Boon Limited

ISBN 0-373-03153-X

Harlequin Romance first edition October 1991

WICKED DECEIVER

CHAPTER ONE

THE man appeared quite suddenly from behind a pillar at the end of the crowded hotel dining-room, directly into Olinda's line of view. Tall, black-haired and as handsome as ever, dressed in an elegant dark grey suit.

He raised one hand and snapped manicured fingers. 'A table for one,' he commanded brusquely.

Seated alone at her corner table, Olinda blinked once, incredulously, and felt her blood turn to ice in her veins. Of all the people she might have prayed not to bump into—here in Miami or anywhere else—Guy de Chevalley was at the very top of her list!

But it was Guy all right. There was no doubt about that. Though six years had passed since their last meeting, there could be no mistaking those chiselled dark features, that powerful physique or that arrogant bearing.

Time had evidently failed to soften him, she observed, just as it had also failed to extinguish the hatred that burned for him deep in her heart.

'Of course, sir. This way, please.'

A waiter was hovering at the Frenchman's elbow, just as waiters had hovered all his life, anxious to do the de Chevalley bidding. With a surge of contempt, Olinda dropped her eyes and, for the millionth time in the past six years, cursed with all her heart the man who had caused such terrible grief to her family.

For it was thanks to Guy de Chevalley, this man whom she had prayed never to set eyes on again, that her sister Dolores, whom she had adored, was dead.

At the memory, pain cut like a knife inside her. All at once, the agony of all those years ago seemed as vivid and real as yesterday. And she cursed him again with redoubled feeling for bringing the past so cruelly back to her. Up until just a minute ago she had been feeling well pleased with her lot in life.

Olinda had flown into the steamy mid-April heat of Miami just a few hours ago, simmering with excitement for the conference ahead and blessing the double-edged twist of fate that had unexpectedly brought her here. Had it not been for the untimely attack of sciatica that had so hopelessly immobilised her boss she would never have been given this chance of a lifetime to represent the company she worked for at one of the foremost conferences on the scientific calendar.

'You deserve it,' Dr Allan had assured her, speaking from his sickbed just two nights ago. 'You're one of our hardest-working young researchers. It's high time you had a taste of some of the perks.'

Olinda knew that he was speaking the truth. It would have been false modesty to deny it. Throughout the four years she had spent with the firm she had put her heart and her soul into her work, anxious to establish herself in her chosen field. And the present conference, though undoubtedly a perk, she had no intention of treating as some junket. On the contrary, she would be taking it very seriously. Then, on her return home, she would present to Dr Allan, along with the other senior directors, a meticulous and impressive report of its findings. This conference, she had decided, could be a godsent opportunity for her to clinch the promotion she was after.

These career-minded thoughts had very nearly dissuaded her from going ahead with her holiday plans. For it had initially struck her that this trip to Miami offered her a truly unrepeatable opportunity to do something really special with the two weeks she had coming. Instead of renting a cottage in Wales, as she had planned, she could extend her three-day stay in Miami by a further two weeks in the nearby Caribbean.

And yet she had dithered, torn by this exotic temptation and the desire to get her conference report in promptly. In the end it was Dr Allan himself who had made up her mind for her. 'You won't have a chance to present your report until two weeks later, anyway,' he'd told her. 'We're going to be busy with a delegation from Japan.'

All the better, Olinda had decided happily. That way I get to have my cake and eat it! And this morning, when she had set off from London's Heathrow Airport, she had believed there was nothing in the world that could possibly spoil her transatlantic stay. But then, of course, she hadn't reckoned on bumping into Guy de Chevalley!

Still, there was at least one thing to be grateful for, she reassured herself, as she averted her eyes. Over the past six years Guy might not have changed, but she herself had altered immeasurably. There was no way he would recognise in the assured young woman she had become the gauche, unsophisticated nineteen-year-old he had met so briefly on his native Corsica.

With any luck, she bent her head and prayed, it might just conceivably be possible for her to see out the three days of the conference without their paths ever having to cross.

But prayers, alas, were not always answered, as fate now lost no time in reminding her. All at once, a shadow fell across her chair. 'Excuse me, *mademoiselle*,' a deep voice charged her. 'You appear to be sitting at my table.'

Startled, Olinda jerked her head up. She had been quite unaware of his approach. '*Your* table?' she challenged, feeling her cheeks glow pink as she looked up, disorientated, into his face.

And what a face! she found herself thinking. The straight patrician nose, the strong square jaw, the curved black brows, like devil's wings. And those eyes—how could she have forgotten those eyes?—of a deep and piercing cobalt blue, startling in their almost ferocious beauty—and fringed with a sweep of thick sooty lashes most women would gladly have sold their souls for.

He smiled, a composed, superior smile, the wide lips describing a haughty curve, yet dimpling sensuously at the corners. 'That's right, *mademoiselle*. This is my table.' Then he paused to fix her with a long, slow glance, the deep blue eyes openly appraising, as they seemed to absorb every detail of her appearance.

They started with her head of wavy light brown hair that fell in soft cascades to her shoulders, paused at the perfect oval of her face with its rosebud mouth and wide grey eyes, at this moment filled with undiluted censure, then caressed the slim, shapely lines of her figure—elegantly clad in a beige linen suit and a simple but effective white cotton blouse—before moving down to the slender crossed legs and the neat tan leather sling-back shoes.

'Not that I have any objection to your sharing it,' he added smoothly, his attention returning once more to her face. 'The company of a young, attractive woman is not something I am ever particularly eager to deny myself.'

So he had not changed in that respect either! The playboy head of the De Chevalley Foundation, renowned for its work in scientific research, was still the shameless womaniser of before! A man who broke hearts without a moment's hesitation, who treated females as a form of cheap entertainment and who possessed not one moral scruple to his name!

Olinda had followed his antics sporadically through the scribblings of the gossip columnists at home, and she knew only too well that her beloved Dolores was far from being the only one whose heart he had broken. This man whose name, publicly, was linked to so much good work, privately had much of which to be ashamed.

Olinda's eyes narrowed with hostility. 'Then I'm afraid the objection must come from me.' The very last thing in the world she wanted was Guy de Chevalley sitting at her table, and she intended making no bones about it. Her tone was clipped as she appealed to the waiter, who, throughout, had continued to hover close by, 'Perhaps you would kindly explain to this gentleman that this is my table and he must find himself another?'

Plainly embarrassed, the waiter cleared his throat.

'I'm sorry, miss, but there's been a mix-up. The gentleman is right. This is his table.'

Olinda flushed irritably and scrambled to her feet, abandoning her half-eaten seafood salad. 'Then kindly show me to mine!' she demanded, keeping her eyes averted from Guy de Chevalley's face—which, though a good half-head higher than her own, suddenly felt much too close. Likewise the broad, white-shirted chest, the hard square shoulders, the long lean legs. By rising to her feet she had diminished the space between them and his sudden nearness was somehow overwhelming. Threatening too, in a subtly sensual way.

And he, she sensed, was equally aware of their sudden state of physical closeness. A potent charge of electricity crackled in the air between them.

The waiter wrung his hands in mortification. 'Alas, miss, no table has been reserved for you. When the booking was changed from Dr Allan's name, some error in the computer must have occurred. You were shown to this table by mistake, and I'm afraid all the other tables are taken.' He glanced appealingly at Guy de Chevalley and then, equally appealingly, back at Olinda. 'However, if you were to accept this gentleman's offer to share his table, the problem would be solved.'

That was what he thought! Her problems would be just beginning! Already, merely through his arrival on the scene, she could feel her appetite for the three days ahead suddenly and abruptly waning. With a stiffening of her vertebrae, she demanded implacably, 'And what if I refuse?'

Miserably, the waiter sucked air between his teeth

and gestured with one hand round the densely-packed dining-room. 'Well, of course, some solution would have to be found, but I'm afraid it would mean sharing with some other guest. . .'

Sharing with the creature from the Black Lagoon would be preferable to sharing with Guy de Chevalley, but Olinda was suddenly acutely conscious that she was making a quite uncharacteristic scene—and that the only one who was suffering as a result was the hapless waiter, whose fault none of this was. Her ungracious response to Guy de Chevalley's offer had turned not one dark hair of the Frenchman's head. In fact, his expression, as she sneaked him a look, only to meet the full beam of the dark cobalt eyes, was one of aloof, superior amusement. This predicament she found herself in evidently appealed to his warped sense of humour.

It would be better, she found herself reluctantly conceding, to bow for the moment to the hand of fate. Unpalatable as it would prove to be, she would survive the ordeal of a dinner with Guy de Chevalley—then in other more discreet and private circumstances she could make alternative arrangements for the remainder of her stay.

As his eyes continued to mesh with hers, just a few feet away, across the table, she reseated herself with a politely resigned sigh and replaced her napkin over her knees. 'Very well. In the circumstances, I agree.'

Relief instantly flooded the waiter's face, as he set about laying a second place. 'A very sensible decision, miss. I'm sure you'll find the arrangement satisfactory.'

Olinda nodded non-committally, knowing differently, and discreetly drew back her knees as Guy de Chevalley sat down opposite, arranging his long legs beneath the table. Then, studiously ignoring him—she would exchange not one word!—she lifted her fork and took a mouthful of her squid.

But he was not about to leave her in peace. As the waiter, for the moment, took his leave, Guy sat back and eyed her over the top of the menu. 'The waiter is right—this is an ideal arrangement. Personally, I hate to eat alone.'

The dark blue eyes with their devil's wing eyebrows regarded her provocatively as he spoke and there was a lightly mocking edge to his voice, almost as though he had read her mind perfectly and was deliberately baiting her. Then one eyebrow lifted interrogatively as he invited her response.

'A bit of company at the dinner table is always welcome, don't you think?'

And he really was quite impossibly handsome, in his insolent and arrogant way. Though she hated him for what he had done to Dolores, Olinda had never had any problem understanding what it was her sister had seen in him. She had always considered that the hapless Dolores, twenty-five years old and already a divorcee when the unfortunate affair with Guy de Chevalley had occurred, had shown a remarkable lack of insight and wisdom in becoming so deeply, so abandonedly involved with such an obviously dangerous man. But on a more basic and instinctive level she could scarcely fault her sister's taste.

As she met his gaze now, her eyes travelled his

features—and perhaps, after all, he had changed a bit. The lines of the handsome, deeply tanned face were a fraction more firmly etched than before, and the hard glint that lurked deep in the blue eyes had grown more ruthless over the years. If she had found him, at thirty, stunning but unscrupulous, she found him even more so now, at thirty-six. Both more unscrupulous and, impossibly, more handsome—and it was the former quality she must keep in mind.

She would be a fool with a very short memory indeed if she were to allow herself to be taken in by his bone-melting blue eyes and seductive smiles!

'It depends on the company,' she shot back icily, finally deigning to answer his question. 'There are times when I prefer to dine alone.'

'Like now, for instance?' he enquired calmly, yet with just the hint of a hard glint in his eyes. 'Even on so brief an acquaintance, you find my company not to your taste?'

That brought her up short. She was handling this badly, sending out signals she did not intend him to receive. If she was to keep her identity a secret and avoid all the anguish that her unmasking would unleash, then she must be at pains to treat him with careful detachment, like the stranger he was supposed to be.

Apologetically, she adjusted her tone and switched on a smile that urged forbearance. 'I'm sorry, I didn't mean to imply any such thing. I don't even know you, as you say. It's just that I'm feeling rather tired and not much in the mood for conversation. I flew in from London just three hours ago.'

He smiled back in response, a smile of understanding, though that hard glint deep in his eyes remained. He was a man, she sensed, who would remember a discourtesy and repay it in full at a time when he chose. For the moment, however, he wore a mask of commiseration. 'Yes, indeed. The transatlantic haul tends to be extremely tiring. I've just endured a similar flight from Paris myself.' His eyes scanned her face as he leaned back a little. 'Are you here for the conference, or just on holiday?'

'Oh, I'm here for the conference,' Olinda assured him, adding with a dismissive little laugh, 'People like me don't come here on holiday. Such luxuries are the preserve of people like yourself.'

She realised her *faux pas* the instant she'd said it. One eyebrow arced in a show of curiosity. The deep cobalt eyes fastened on her face. 'People like me?' Guy paused significantly. 'What exactly do you mean by that?'

For a moment Olinda hesitated, cursing herself for this second clumsy gaffe. Then, on an impulse, deciding to bluff it out—after all, what other choice did she have?—she pushed a soft curl back from her face and looked directly into his eyes.

'Well, of course, I'm only guessing,' she began, her tone mock-innocent, deliberately tentative, 'but to look at you I'd say you're a very wealthy man.' Her eyes rested pointedly on the cashmere suit, the made-to-measure shirt, the designer silk tie, then drifted downwards to the solid gold cufflinks, and the long-fingered, shapely, manicured hands. 'Forgive me for being personal, but you definitely have an air of wealth about you.'

Plus the insensitivity and arrogance that go with such privilege, she added maliciously to herself, as the waiter chose that moment to arrive at their table to take Guy de Chevalley's order. But she continued to hold her smile convincingly as he ordered, then paused to consider his answer.

'I had no idea I was being studied so closely.' He held her eyes steadily, his gaze boring into her, making her feel that once again he had read into her mind. Then the wide lips curved as he continued, 'However, I have no objection whatsoever to your getting personal. Feel free to get as personal as you please, Miss——' He interrupted the oddly barbed invitation and leaned across the table towards her, the expression in the blue eyes dark and unfathomable. 'I'm afraid I don't know your name. Perhaps it's time we introduced ourselves.'

Olinda swallowed. This was the moment of truth. Either she must lie to maintain her anonymity or bank on her suspicion that, in the course of her relationship with him, Dolores was unlikely ever to have mentioned her little sister's proper name. On that brief, ill-starred visit to Corsica, Olinda had been introduced to him as Lulu, the baby name that had stuck with her right up into her teens—and there was the added camouflage of the fact that Dolores had been known by her married name of Reid. It was possible that he had forgotten—if indeed it had ever entered his consciousness—what his jilted girlfriend's maiden name had been.

She decided to take a gamble. A man like Guy de

Chevalley was unlikely to remember the minor, extraneous details of so insignificant an episode in his life. With a toss of her head she straightened and told him, 'My name is Olinda Steven.'

There now, it was out! Let him make what he would of it!

An enigmatic simle touched his lips. 'Olinda? An unusual name.' As his eyes scanned her face, she felt herself tense. Heaven forbid that he should associate Olinda with Lulu! Then, with an inward sigh, she relaxed as he added, 'I don't believe I've ever heard it before. It suits you. It's very pretty.'

She lowered her eyes to hide her relief. 'Thank you,' she murmured.

'And I'm Guy de Chevalley,' he informed her unnecessarily, forcing her to look up at him again. He held out his hand, and as it clasped hers she felt for one sharply disconcerting moment the firm, warm pressure of his flesh against hers. He had a masterful handshake, crisp and domineering. She found herself snatching her hand away.

'In case you're wondering,' he added, smiling, making mocking allusion to her failure to ask, 'I'm over here for the conference too. I'm hoping it will throw up something of interest. I'm in the business of scientific research.'

It was a perfect opening. Too good to let pass. Olinda regarded him ultra-casually, play-acting to the hilt with her eyes. 'You're not connected with the De Chevalley Foundation, by any chance, are you?' she enquired.

He nodded. 'Indeed I am. Its founder, Louise de Chevalley, was my grandmother, as a matter of fact.'

With an effort Olinda forced her features to look suitably impressed. After all, she had been impressed once. As an innocent, unworldly sixth-former, contemplating a career in chemistry, she had been quite overawed when her clever, bilingual sister had announced that she had just landed a job as personal assistant to the brilliant young chairman of the De Chevalley Foundation.

But her feelings on the subject had changed radically since then. Though she continued to admire the work of the Foundation, which stood at the very forefront of scientific research, Dolores' ultimately fatal experience had taught Olinda nothing but hatred for its cold-hearted chairman. She lowered her eyes now lest her feelings might show, and felt almost grateful when he asked, 'So tell me, Olinda, what kind of work are you involved in?'

'Pharmaceuticals,' she told him sparsely, for once unwilling to be drawn into a deeper discussion of the work she loved. 'I'm a senior research assistant with a small drugs company in the south of England.'

'Is this your first conference? I haven't seen you around before.' Then, before she could answer, he added, 'One tends to see the same old faces over and over again at these things. It makes rather a pleasant change to see some new young faces on the scene.'

'So you're a regular conference-goer, are you?' She ignored the flattery and fixed him with a look. 'I'm surprised that the boss of so large a company has time to indulge in such pursuits.'

'I like to keep abreast of what my counterparts around the world are doing. And as a forum for meeting people and exchanging ideas nothing can really beat these conferences.'

I'll bet! she thought with a cynical twist. Not to mention also the opportunities they create for meeting lots of new young faces! The redoubtable Guy de Chevalley, with his taste for innocent, easy victims, would not hesitate, she felt certain, to abuse his exalted position at such events in order to add a few more female scalps to his belt!

She regarded him darkly as the waiter arrived with his first course and her entrée and laid the two plates on the table before them. Well, at least such pursuits would keep him out of her hair, she thought to herself with dour satisfaction. For he must surely have got the message by now that he would be seriously wasting his time if he had any thoughts of setting his sights on her!

As the thought crossed her mind, she had to confess to a secret desire that he might be rash enough to try. It would give her an enormous amount of satisfaction to hand out a taste of sexual rejection to the almighty, womanising Guy de Chevalley. Though, regrettably, it would be beyond her powers to match the calculated cruelty he had dished out to Dolores.

They ate in silence for a while, Olinda watching him from beneath lowered lashes as he finished his starter and set about his steak. The man had a formidable appetite, she observed—for good food as well as for pretty women.

It was just as he was pouring them each more wine that the waiter suddenly appeared at his elbow. 'There's a call for you, Mr de Chevalley. Will you take it at the counter or at your table?'

'I'll take it here,' Guy nodded, casting a faintly mocking glance at Olinda. 'I'm sure the young lady won't object?'

'Not in the slightest,' Olinda assured him sarcastically. At least, if he were to spend the rest of the meal on the telephone, she would be spared the inconvenience of having to converse with him.

As it was, the phone call was all too brief. Less than a couple of minutes later he was handing the phone back to the waiter and extracting from his pocket a tiny personal tape-recorder into which he dictated a brief message and a phone number.

'A quite invaluable *aide-mémoire*,' he observed to Olinda as he laid it to one side on the table. 'I find that messages scribbled on bits of paper invariably tend to get mislaid.'

'How inconvenient.' She smiled back at him thinly. 'Losing phone numbers, especially those important ones, can seriously cramp one's style.'

She thought she saw a glimmer of a smile, as though he had perfectly understood her innuendo. Then he raised one devil's wing eyebrow and enquired, 'Are you planning to go straight back to England after the conference?'

Why did he ask? 'As a matter of fact, no.' Olinda shook her head and held his eyes. Whatever strange thought might have entered his head, he would not be adding *her* number to his list. In a cool tone she informed him, 'I'm planning to spend a couple of weeks lying on a beach in Barbados first.'

He raised one dark eyebrow at her. 'I thought you

told me earlier that such luxuries were beyond the reach of people like you?'

'Normally, yes.' So he had remembered her gibe! 'But since I'm already in the area, I discovered I could do it relatively cheaply—for little more than I'd pay for a package holiday to Spain.' She wrinkled her shapely nose at him and added, 'Of course, the hotel I'll be staying at is a modest little establishment, not one of those flashy five-star jobs that people like yourself frequent.'

'As long as it's clean and free from vermin, there's no reason why it shouldn't suit your needs. . .' With a smile that was evidently intended to unnerve her, Guy let his voice trail off. He took a leisurely mouthful of his wine, then added in an ominous tone, 'You've had it thoroughly checked out, of course?'

'You mean it might not be. . .clean and. . .free from vermin?' The very possibility appalled her. Even the words seemed to stick in her throat.

And Guy de Chevalley was not in the market to reassure her. 'In that part of the world, it's always possible. Though you're really unlikely to be troubled by anything more serious than a couple of cockroaches.'

'Cockroaches?' Olinda suppressed a shudder. 'Don't tell me they get into people's bedrooms?'

'They get everywhere, my dear Olinda. But though they're big—sometimes extremely so—they're perfectly harmless, I assure you. Just keep a couple of cans of pesticide by your bed and you should manage to keep them under control.'

Under control! Just how many of the ghastly creatures was he suggesting she might expect?

Olinda shivered beneath her beige linen jacket, as she forced herself to meet his blue gaze. He was doing this deliberately, of course. In his subtle, sophisticated way, repaying her for her earlier rudeness. And he could scarcely have selected a more effective weapon. Olinda's horror of creepy-crawlies was legendary among her friends!

It was at that moment, as she fell into a stricken silence, that the waiter came to remove their plates. She could feel Guy's eyes fixed amusedly on her face, evidently relishing the ashen pallor his unkind words had brought to her cheeks. And she was ninety-nine point nine per cent certain that he failed to notice the waiter's accidental slip that sent the tape recorder with a soft thud to the floor. She might not even have been aware of it herself were it not for the fact that it happened to land less than a centimetre away from her foot.

For an instant she almost bent to retrieve it and return it to its owner, but she paused as with that look of superior composure Guy went on to say, 'If such things trouble you so deeply, you should stick to Europe for your adventures. My own island, Corsica, for example. We have our share of bugs, of course, but they tend to be on a lesser scale.' His eyes scanned her face, holding her gaze for a moment. 'Have you ever been there?' he enquired.

All thoughts and fears of creepy-crawlies had suddenly vanished from Olinda's head. All she was aware of was the tape recorder and the sudden rash impulse that filled her. She continued to stare across at him and demanded stupidly, 'Have I ever been where?'

'Corsica.'

'Ah. . .Corsica! No, I haven't,' she lied. Then she added with an automatic smile, as a sudden idea began to take shape, 'I really ought to go some time. I believe it's a very beautiful island.'

'Extremely so. And if you should ever visit, I would be honoured to be your host.'

Would he indeed? Well, that would never happen! Once had already been more than enough.

She feigned appreciation. 'That's very kind. I must remember to keep your offer in mind.' With a subtle movement under the table, she nudged the tape recorder with her foot a little closer to her bag, which lay beside her on the floor. Then she flexed her shoulders and stifled a yawn. 'I think it's time I called it a day. If you don't mind, I'll leave you now.'

As he nodded, 'You go ahead,' she bent down to pick up her bag from the floor and there, exactly in her line of vision, lay Guy de Chevalley's shiny silver tape recorder.

For a heartbeat she paused. What she was planning was wrong. But then she thought of Corsica and Dolores and all the bitter, cruel memories he had brought flooding back, and with a small squeeze of triumph she reached out her hand and closed it around the cool metal object. A moment later she had dropped it into her bag and with commendable composure was rising to her feet.

'It's been very nice meeting you, Mr de Chevalley. I hope you enjoy the conference.'

'I'm sure I shall.' He held her eyes. 'And I look forward to seeing you at breakfast tomorrow.'

Not if I see you first, you won't! She bit back the

temptation to say it out loud, as she swung her bag casually over her shoulder, and made do instead with a brisk, 'Goodnight.'

Then she was heading across the crowded dining-room, her heart beating like a drum inside her chest, almost as though some sixth sense was telling her how bitterly she would live to regret the rash and foolish thing that she had just done.

CHAPTER TWO

IT HAD never for one moment been Olinda's intention to steal Guy de Chevalley's tape recorder, nor even less to listen to what might be on it. The sudden impulse that had spurred her to take it had been formed of a simple desire to thwart him. Puny gesture though it was, it had seemed like a small way of getting back at him. For suddenly, at his casual mention of Corsica, she had been filled with an angry, dark need for revenge.

Out of the dining-room, as she waited for the lift to carry her to her room on the twenty-second floor, she was amazed that she had carried off the feat so unemotionally, for, inwardly, she had been feeling far from unemotional. The memories that his mention of Corsica had rekindled still had her quivering inside.

She stepped into the lift and allowed the doors to swallow her, as she pressed the button for her floor. Call this revenge? she challenged herself bitterly, as she was instantly, silently borne aloft. This impetuous and pathetic gesture scarcely merited the name of revenge! All she had in fact done, most probably, was deprive him temporarily of a couple of phone numbers!

Up in her room she dumped her bag and its contents contemptuously in a corner of the dressing-table. Really, if this was the best she could manage by way of getting even on behalf of her sister, she would have been better to leave well alone. Considering what Dolores had suffered, it was almost an insult to her memory.

She kicked off her shoes and shrugged off her jacket, then picked up the phone and called down to room service. 'A glass of warm milk, please,' she requested. Perhaps that would soothe her and help her to sleep.

With a disgruntled sigh she unzipped her skirt, stepped out of it and tossed it on to a chair. In all probability it would take much more than a simple glass of warm milk to soothe her, and she knew she was unlikely to sleep a wink. That encounter with Guy de Chevalley had upset her badly. She was still mentally reeling from the shock of it.

She cast a guilty glance at her bag on the dressing-table. She had been mad, nevertheless, to take the tape recorder—whichever way you cared to look at it. For the harsh truth was it was downright ludicrous even to think in terms of revenge. Men like Guy de Chevalley sailed blithely through life without anyone ever seriously challenging their behaviour. They were the devil's anointed, beyond human accountability, destined never—in this life, at least—to pay the price of their misdeeds.

Irritably, Olinda tugged her white blouse over her head. And of such men there appeared to be no shortage. Her very own father had been one, walking out on his wife and two small daughters more than twenty years ago.

And, of course, more recently, there had been Julian.

She pushed the thought away as bitter memories flickered through her. Julian was her past, but he still served as a reminder of the cold-hearted callousness of which men could be capable. Though in a league table of callousness she doubted very much that he would come anywhere near the Frenchman, Guy de Chevalley.

With a sigh Olinda reached for the white cotton robe that she had earlier hung up in the cupboard and slipped it on quickly before crossing to the bathroom. The more she thought about it, the more she realised how foolish she had been to risk tangling with de Chevalley. Taking the tape recorder had been sheer unbridled folly, and she would be wise now to get it back to him as quickly as possible—and preferably without him ever suspecting the part she had played in its disappearance.

She pulled the belt of the thin cotton robe tightly around her slim waist and bent to turn on the hot water tap. She could think about how she might accomplish that task while she relaxed in a steamy-hot bubble bath, sipping the glass of warm milk she had ordered.

As a sharp tap sounded on the bedroom door, Olinda smiled to herself and straightened. Room service had been impressively quick with her order.

'Coming!' she called out, as another knock sounded. Then hugging her thin cotton robe around her, she pulled open the door with a grateful smile. But her smile shrivelled like a punctured balloon at the vision that met her startled gaze.

'We meet again.' His tone was not friendly. There was an ominous look in the cobalt blue eyes. 'I had not expected this pleasure so soon.'

It was Olinda's immediate reaction to slam the door shut in his face—she did not care for that glint in his eye that reflected anything but pleasure. But something about the set of the tall, muscular frame, that seemed almost threateningly to fill the doorway, caused her fingers to freeze immobile on the door-handle. Almost certainly his reflexes would be faster than her own. He would have forced the door back open before she had it half shut, and she had not the faintest desire for this encounter to get physical.

So instead she inched it closed just a fraction, as though in modest protection of her scanty attire. 'I'm afraid you've caught me at a most inconvenient moment. I was just about to have a bath,' she told him.

Any faint hope that he might take the hint abruptly evaporated as he took a step forward. And she had been right about those lightning reflexes. His hand was on the door, propping it open, almost before she was aware of him moving. 'First things first.' He looked her straight in the eye. 'I believe you are in possession of something of mine?'

At that point there were two clear options open to her. She could confess on the spot, beg his forgiveness and give him back his wretched tape recorder. Or she could deny all knowledge of what he was talking about and pray that she could convince him of her innocence. As she looked up into those unforgiving eyes, it took her less than a second to make her choice.

Deliberately, Olinda furrowed her brow. 'I'm afraid I have no idea what you're talking about,' she told him, somehow managing to meet the sabre-like gaze. To confess would simply be to invite serious trouble. It would be safer to try and bluff it out.

'Oh, no?' His tone was patently disbelieving. 'What

I'm talking about, Miss Steven, is the tape recorder you so cleverly walked off with.'

'Tape recorder?' Her brow furrowed more deeply. 'Whatever makes you think I took your tape recorder?' She tried an innocent, dismissive laugh. 'I have no use for your tape recorder, Mr de Chevalley.' If she stuck to her guns, he would have no choice but to back off and take her word for it. Then first thing tomorrow she would devise a plan to get the confounded instrument back to him.

The blue eyes were still on her and their expression had not softened. 'So you deny that you took it?'

'Of course I deny it!'

'Miss Steven, I see you are not only a thief, you are also a shameless, if incompetent, liar!' Then, before she could give voice to the words of protest that were forming indignantly on her lips, he had pushed the door wide, sending her staggering backwards, and was barging angrily into the room.

He stood in the middle of the room, like an unleashed fury from the pit of hell, blue eyes blazing like incandescent torches, the furious energy that seemed to radiate from every pore of him threatening to send the whole room up in flames. His gaze swivelled searchingly this way and that. 'Kindly tell me what you've done with it!'

'I've told you already, I haven't done anything with it! And what right do you think you have to come barging in here?'

'Ah!' Suddenly his eyes fell on the bag on the dressing-table and in a couple of strides he had crossed over to grab hold of it. Utterly aghast, feeling her insides turn to sawdust, Olinda watched as he snatched the zip open, then an instant later the blood drained from her veins as he turned once more towards her, holding the tape recorder aloft.

'So you don't know anything about it, do you not?' His tone was sheared metal as he tossed the bag aside. 'Then kindly explain how it came to be here!'

Olinda had stopped breathing. She felt suddenly faint. 'I don't know,' she stammered. 'I swear I don't know.'

'More lies, I see.' He had come to stand before her. 'In addition to being a thief and liar, you are also, I see, a pathetic little coward. At least have the dignity to own up to what you've done!'

And have him tear her limb from limb on the spot? She swallowed drily and offered nervously, 'It must have fallen off the table into my bag—without my noticing.' She twitched a nervous smile. 'That's the only explanation I can think of.'

'And a pretty poor explanation it is. You don't seriously expect me to believe it?' As he spoke, his eyes pierced through her like lances, as cold and impersonal as twin blades of steel. 'If you take me for some kind of fool, Miss Steven, you're making a very big mistake.'

That much she knew. Guy de Chevalley was no fool. A callous philanderer and an arrogant bully, but with a dangerously sharp and incisive intelligence. She would have to do better than that to convince him.

But her poor, shell-shocked brain could come up with nothing, however hard she urged it to struggle. She tried a new tactic. 'Why won't you believe me? What could I possibly want with your tape recorder?'

'That one's easy enough to answer.' He smiled a grim smile, as he continued to glare down at her. 'There are various bits of information on that tape that might well be of interest to fellow scientists. As I told you, I use the tape as an *aide-mémoire*, for storing ideas as well as phone numbers.' He paused and fixed her with a steely cold look. 'Is that the reason you took it, Miss Steven? Are you some kind of industrial spy?' he accused.

'Good heavens, no! What a preposterous idea!'

'I'm afraid I don't find it preposterous in the least. On the contrary, I consider it the most likely explanation. Unless you can come up with a better one, of course.'

Olinda was almost tempted to tell him the truth— that she had simply done it out of aimless spite—but the truth could lead her into all sorts of difficulties and the sort of explanations she was anxious to avoid. In a small, sincere voice she hastened to assure him, 'Whatever else I am, I'm not a spy.'

'You mean you confess to being a thief and a liar, but you expect me to believe that you're not a spy?'

'I didn't say that. I didn't confess anything. But I can assure you, absolutely, I'm not a spy.'

He looked down at her for a long, burning moment. 'We shall see how convinced others may be by your denial, Miss Steven. I for one remain thoroughly sceptical.' Very pointedly, he held up the tape recorder, flicked the off switch and returned it to his pocket. Then, as she followed the performance with horror-stricken gaze, he added unnecessarily and with sadistic pleasure, 'As you see, our entire conversation has been taped.'

If Olinda had been feeling shell-shocked before, now she felt as though a mine had just blown up in her face. She stared at him blankly for a moment. 'Why did you tape it?' she demanded shakily.

'For evidence.' He smiled a shark-like smile. 'To use against you, if I should so decide.'

Olinda swallowed, tasting bile. 'To use against me—how?' she croaked.

He shrugged. 'I could have you thrown out of the conference, for a start.' Holding her gaze, he raised his fingers and snapped them demonstratively in her face. 'Just like that. In two minutes flat.' As he paused, his lips quirked with pure malicious pleasure. 'If I were so minded, I could probably even have you thrown out of your job.'

Olinda had frozen, speechless, to the spot. Her mouth opened and shut, but no sound came out. How was it possible that, through one foolish move, she had brought down on her head this unspeakable catastrophe?

'But I fear you have a more immediate problem. . .' All at once, he was glancing away, his eyes swivelling abruptly in the direction of the bathroom. 'If I'm not mistaken, I can hear running water.'

The bath! She had left the hot tap running, completely forgetting it in the midst of all her traumas.

With a strangled yelp she turned on her heel and went bounding off towards the bathroom. The whole place was probably flooded by now! And, as she went rocketing through the doorway, she could see she was right. Hot water in a steamy waterfall was emptying over the edge of the bath and the tiled floor was already two inches deep.

Alas, not quite enough to drown oneself in, she thought to herself with a twist of black humour, as she waded to the bath and turned off the tap. Cruel fate, it seemed, had even denied her this convenient exit from her sudden predicament—though there was always the water in the bath itself should she fancy scalding herself to death instead!

'A bit of a mess.' The tall figure in the doorway was surveying the damage with an unconcerned eye. 'But don't worry,' he observed practically, 'it'll clear itself up.' He pointed to a small round metal grille in the middle of the blue-tiled floor. 'The drain will swallow most of it. The best thing you can do is just leave it for a while.'

His even, sensible reaction had instantly allayed her moment of panic, and Olinda could see that he was right. The drain was already gurgling greedily as the swirling flood went pouring down it. She threw him an oblique look, feeling glad he'd been around—then instantly realised how idiotic that was. The accident would never have happened if it hadn't been for him distracting her!

Her mind jerked back miserably to the tape recorder, as she snatched a bath towel from the rail and followed him back into the bedroom. If only she'd had the common sense to think ahead to the consequences of her actions! She dried her sopping feet and tossed the towel on to the bed. After all, she had not exactly been unaware of the ruthless disposition of the man with whom she was dealing!

As she lifted her gaze, he was standing there watching her, holding out a tall glass of milk. 'Room service brought this while you were in the bathroom. You'd better drink it while it's still hot.'

Such solicitude! Olinda took the warm glass, careful to avoid his fingers as she did so. There was something a little disorientating, she was thinking, as she laid the glass on the bedside table, about this uncanny ability he had to deal on two different levels at once. One minute he was the raging tyrant, the next dishing out advice on flooded bathrooms and expressing concern about her milk. She turned back to look at him, her expression shuttered, wondering which side of him she would be presented with next.

'As I was saying——' He had returned to being the tyrant. His eyes, once more, were as hard as boulders '—I could make a great deal of trouble for you should I so wish.'

It had never crossed her mind to question that. De Chevalley was a man of considerable power and influence and, thanks to that inept denial which he had so thoughtfully taped, she had virtually condemned herself out of her own mouth. It would be all too easy for him to have her thrown out of the conference.

Her heart turned over sickly. What a disgrace! And though he had probably been exaggerating just a bit when he had threatened that he could also have her thrown out of her job—she was, after all, highly thought of by her company—he undoubtedly had the power to scupper her promotion, and that would be quite bad enough.

Inwardly she felt herself sag. 'And do you so wish?' she enquired tentatively.

He gave her a long look. 'I have not yet decided.' Then he patted the pocket where he had slipped the tape recorder, and smiled sadistically, deliberately torturing her. 'As long as I keep the evidence safe, I can decide in good time how best to use it. Who knows?' The blue eyes flickered warningly. 'It might prove to be in my best interests to keep what has happened between ourselves.'

Olinda felt a cold finger trickle down her spine. Was this a subtle hint at blackmail? She regarded him narrowly through steady grey eyes. 'If you're thinking of trying a bit of extortion, I can promise you now it would be a total waste of time. I haven't any money to pay you.'

De Chevalley smiled again without humour, then turned almost contemptuously towards the door. 'Don't worry, I have no need of your money. I already have more than enough of my own.' He paused for a moment, his hand on the door-handle, and allowed his eyes to sweep languidly over her. 'But perhaps you have other assets that might interest me.'

As she burned beneath that gaze that seemed to strip her naked, he pulled the door open and stepped out into the corridor. 'When I have come to my decision, I shall let you know. For the moment, *chérie*, enjoy your freedom.'

Enjoyment of anything was suddenly beyond her. Even when, at last, she climbed into the bathtub, the warm, frothy water closing soothingly around her, Olinda could not shake the heaviness from her heart.

It was cruel beyond belief that Guy de Chevalley should have come barging into her life like this, casting his dark shadow over not only the present but over her very future as well. Hadn't he already done enough in the past?

She lay back in the bubbles and closed her eyes. Hadn't he inflicted enough damage on her family to last them all a hundred hurtful lifetimes?

As pain and anger shuddered through her, her mind went flying back to Corsica and that summer six years ago when her sister's tragedy had begun.

They had flown over for a holiday, Olinda and her mother, on Dolores' excited insistence. The romance that had been flowering between her and Guy for months, since soon after she had gone to work for him, looked poised for a traditional happy ending. Just a few weeks earlier Dolores had written to say that they were soon to be engaged.

Naturally, they had both been delighted for Dolores. Olinda's glamorous, adventurous, blonde-haired sister, so different from Olinda in every way, was overdue a bit of happiness in her personal life. Just a year before, her short-lived marriage had ended in divorce, and before that there had been a string of broken romances, which, although she had joked about them, must have hurt. It had been good to know she had found true love at last.

But Olinda had been forced to revise that judgement more or less from day one of that fateful holiday.

For a start, on their arrival, there had been no sign

of Guy. 'I think he's nervous about meeting you both,' Dolores had offered, clearly nervous herself. 'Don't worry, he'll show up tomorrow.'

And indeed he had, quite unexpectedly, surprising the three of them over lunch and insisting with a great deal of charm that he treat them all to dinner that evening. And dinner had been a lavish affair, with Guy an attentive and generous host—though Olinda had watched with disapproval the mechanical way he treated Dolores. Of the adoration she could see shining from her sister's eyes, she could glimpse not the faintest reflection in his.

Likewise not a trace was evident of the nervousness attributed to him by Dolores. Guy de Chevalley, Olinda had rapidly judged, was a man whose nerves were made of iron, not a variety known much to trouble their owner. Of the three of them she was undoubtedly the least surprised by the disaster that unfolded the following evening.

He had told them calmly that he would be busy next evening and suggested they all take dinner together at Olinda and her mother's hotel. As it transpired, they very nearly had, but the hand of fate had intervened.

'Name me the best fish restaurant on the island!' Olinda had challenged her sister on a whim. And when Dolores answered, she had instantly insisted, 'Let's go there tonight instead. My treat!' It had merely been her intention to cheer up Dolores and chase the sad, neglected look from her eyes. She could never have guessed in a million years the agony the evening would bring.

They had barely been in the restaurant half an hour when Guy had walked in with a girl on his arm.

He had appeared not to notice Dolores at first—which was really not so terribly surprising, considering how engrossed he was in his partner. All the enchantment that was so notably lacking when he was in the company of the woman he had promised to marry shone now, unashamedly, from his face.

Olinda had watched in agonised impotence as the colour had drained from her sister's cheeks and she was forced by the uncontrollable tremor of her hands to abandon all efforts with her knife and fork. Then, clumsily, she had stumbled to her feet. 'Excuse me,' she had mumbled to Olinda and her mother. 'I'm sorry, but I can't stay here.' A moment later she was staggering for the door, her eyes haunted with pain and brimming with tears, leaving Olinda and her mother stranded at the table.

It was only then that Guy had appeared to notice what was going on. His eyes snapped from the retreating figure of Dolores to the two numb-faced figures still seated at the table and, for a fraction of a second, Olinda remembered, his face showed some signs of fleeting remorse. Then the expression had vanished, to be replaced by one of cool and arrogant indifference.

That was the moment when she had begun to hate him. Had it not been for her mother's timely entreaty—'I think we ought to leave now too'—she would gladly have crossed the restaurant and torn him to pieces with her bare hands.

Of course, the holiday was ruined. Dolores spent the next few days in tears, and for the remainder of

Olinda's and her mother's stay on the island Guy de
Chevalley had kept out of their way. And though
Olinda had never set eyes on him again—until chance
had chosen to bring them together in the restaurant of
a Miami hotel—she had never forgotten and never
forgiven, and she hated him now as fiercely as then.

Soon after that Dolores had returned to England and
struggled on bravely for almost a year. But she had
been dead inside. She had died that day in Corsica. The
rest had merely been a matter of time.

Olinda bit her lip to stifle a sob now as she remembered that day, just over five years ago, when they had
phoned to tell her that Dolores was dead. She had been
found alone in her apartment, her young life snuffed
out by an overdose of sleeping pills. And at the terrible
news Olinda had breathed a curse on the name of Guy
de Chevalley. For he was the one who had killed her
sister, as surely as if he had shot her through the head.

And in all these years he had never contacted the
family to offer his condolences. Though he must have
learned of Dolores' death and known in his heart that
he had driven her to it. For the cruel truth was that he
hadn't cared. He'd had better things to do with his time
than waste it in grief and bitter remorse.

Olinda shivered now, in spite of the warm water, and
hugged her arms protectively around her. This was the
ruthless manner of man into whose clutches she had
fallen. It was little wonder her heart trembled inside
her to think of the evil that he might do to her.

Olinda slept briefly and fitfully that night, and the very
first image that flashed into her brain, as she stirred

into consciousness early next morning, was the sinister dark image of Guy de Chevalley.

Damn him! She blinked her eyes open, thrust back the bed clothes and sprang determinedly out of bed. Let him breathe down her neck if he wished. She must not allow him to haunt her like this!

She yanked open the curtains and breathed in deeply, as she gazed out at the shimmering palm trees below. He had told her to enjoy her freedom while it lasted, and that was precisely what she was going to do!

She turned away and headed for the bathroom and a shower. Besides, who was to say Guy would carry out his threat to have her thrown out of the conference, or worse? It had probably just been idle talk, spoken in the heat of anger. She slipped off her nightdress, shook back her hair and stepped beneath the invigorating jet. He would have better things to do with his time than bother about her. As long as she was careful to stay out of his way, she would probably be safe enough.

Encouraged by this line of thought, she ordered breakfast in her room, and after waffles and syrup and a jug of coffee she was feeling decidedly less nervous about things. For it had also occurred to her that she held a card in her hand that in any battle between them could prove invaluable. She knew who he was and what he had done to Dolores, whereas he was quite unaware of her identity.

She had no idea how she might use this advantage, only that she intended hanging on to it. Who knew?— it might even enable her finally to turn the tables on him!

After breakfast she dressed in a flattering cream skirt

and blue and cream top and hurried downstairs for the first lecture of the day. She had planned to stop off to see the Dining-Room Manager and sort out the problem of her table, but in the end she decided she didn't have time. She would do that later, during the lunch break. In the meantime, she would do her best to stay as far away from de Chevalley as possible. Preferably at the opposite end of the lecture hall!

Luckily, her eyes fell on him the very first instant she walked through the door.

He was seated in the front row, dressed in a mid-blue suit and sharp white shirt, looking as stunning and as arrogant as ever.

He had his back to her as she walked into the hall, his dark head bent nonchalantly, as he studied some papers, while simultaneously conducting a conversation with the balding, bespectacled man at his side. And Olinda felt her insides squeeze with dislike as he glanced round to make some comment to his companion and she caught a quick glimpse of his profile.

The strong, straight nose, down which he looked at the world, the ultra-masculine, aggressively moulded chin and the high, intelligent brow with its devil's wing eyebrows beneath a head of stunningly sleek black hair. It was cruel and highly unethical of Mother Nature to have endowed such wanton physical perfection on so patently imperfect a man!

The first lecture, by a Director of Research from Düsseldorf in Germany, was absolutely riveting.

'If this is the level of stuff we can expect, I must say I'm really glad I came.'

As the applause in the hall began to die down, Olinda

turned towards her neighbour who had just spoken to her and found herself looking into a pair of brown eyes in a boyishly open and friendly face.

'Hi, I'm Elliot from Philadelphia,' he told her, cheerfully offering her his hand. Then he turned to the redhaired young man at his side. 'And this is Gerry. He's from Boston.'

There was something about them that made her respond to them instantly—a simplicity and an openness that were profoundly refreshing. 'Pleased to meet you. I'm Olinda from England.' She shook hands warmly. 'I was just thinking the same as you. That was a pretty stimulating talk we just heard.'

'I reckon the next one should be pretty good too. The guy who's giving it has had to fill in at short notice for someone else who had to drop out. I heard him before, a couple of years ago. He's a guy who really knows his stuff.' Elliot broke off and glanced at his watch. 'We've got half an hour before it starts. How about joining us for a coffee?'

'I'd love to.' Olinda didn't hesitate. After all, there was safety in numbers. Guy de Chevalley wasn't nearly so likely to accost her while she was in the company of others—and anyway, she liked the look of her new friends. 'Lead the way,' she responded, rising to her feet. 'I'm dying for a cup of coffee!'

It proved to be a thoroughly pleasant half-hour. Elliot and Gerry, she discovered, worked in a similar field to her own and so the three of them had plenty to talk about, and the two boys were easy, undemanding company. When the bell rang and they made their way back to their seats, Olinda was feeling relaxed and restored—and, what was more, she had solved the problem of her dining-room table. As soon as she had mentioned her dilemma—needless to say omitting any reference to Guy de Chevalley—Elliot and Gerry had invited her to join theirs.

As she settled back happily to hear the next lecture, she had momentarily forgotten de Chevalley's existence—but then Elliot poked her in the arm.

'That's him—that's the guy I told you about. The one who's had to fill in for the guy who dropped out.'

Curious, Olinda raised her eyes to the platform as a burst of spontaneous applause broke out—and instantly her heart gave a sickening little lurch and her smile sagged wanly at the corners.

Of course. It had to be. Who else but Guy de Chevalley? She might have guessed that there was no escape, that she was destined to have the wretched man inflicted upon her endlessly!

Tight-lipped, resenting the swelling applause that cascaded enthusiastically round the huge hall, she watched as his tall, commanding figure strode confidently across the stage to the lectern. Did nothing faze Guy de Chevalley? she wondered with intense irritation, as the applause died at last and he proceeded to speak, to her ever-growing chagrin, without a single note. Didn't anything, even fractionally, ever throw him? Was he ever anything other than in total control?

If he was, he was not about to give a demonstration now. For the next hour he held his audience spellbound with a professionally consummate performance. Even Olinda, as she reluctantly joined in the thunderous applause at the end of his lecture, was deeply, though grudgingly, impressed. His reputation, professionally, was deserved. He had not just come to add scalps to his belt!

'Didn't I tell you he was good?' Elliot leaned across and shouted in her ear.

Olinda nodded. 'Yes, you told me,' she answered, carefully noncommittal, all the while wishing to herself, as she watched de Chevalley vacate the platform and return once more to his seat at the front, that his audience knew the man who lurked behind the façade. It was, after all, neither right nor proper for an unprincipled scoundrel like Guy de Chevalley to be held in such universally high regard.

Elliot broke through her thoughts again as he laid a friendly hand on her arm. 'Well, that's the last lecture for this morning. Let's go through now and have lunch.'

'A good idea,' Olinda agreed, feeling a warm, victorious glow spread through her to think of Guy de Chevalley waiting in vain for her to join him at his table.

'Let's try and make it to the dining-room before everybody else descends on it,' Elliot advised, as they all stood up. Then, checking over his shoulder that Olinda was right behind him, he started heading behind Gerry for the door.

It was the bottleneck at the exit that was to blame. Just for a moment, as the crowd converged, Olinda became separated from her new friends. Then, as the mass ahead of her spilled out into the corridor, the two young Americans were swallowed from her sight. Damn! she cursed, her eyes scouring the sea of faces. Where the devil had they disappeared to?

'You're looking for me?'

As a hand touched her arm, she spun round in confusion, half expecting to see Elliot or Gerry at her side. Instead, to her total consternation, she found herself looking into a too-familiar face and a pair of long-lashed cobalt blue eyes.

'No, I'm most certainly not looking for you!' Indignantly, Olinda took a hasty step back and collided clumsily with a man in the crowd. She staggered wildly for a second, as her balance was thrown and she started to fall, but was saved as a strong hand reached out in time and set her securely back on her feet.

She did not like the feel of his hand on her skin. It made her flesh scorch as though touched by a branding iron. She tried to pull away, but he held her securely. 'Come. Allow me to accompany you safely out of this crowd.'

Before she could argue, he was propelling her through the doorway and out into the corridor that led to the lobby. 'I missed you at breakfast,' he was saying. 'Most disappointing. Did you oversleep?'

'No, as a matter of fact, I had breakfast in my room.' She spun round to glare at him as they reached the end of the corridor. 'And now, if you would kindly let me go, I happen to have an appointment for lunch.'

'Indeed you have.' His grip did not slacken. 'You have an appointment with *me*, *chérie*. You will, of course, be having lunch at my table.'

She felt her heart plummet. 'That's where you're wrong,' she started gamely to protest, though already she could sense it was an utter waste of time.

Guy cut straight in, 'I would advise you not to argue. Remember our conversation of last night.'

Olinda was aware of an involuntary tremor. So her assumption that his threats had not really been serious had been nothing but wishful thinking on her part. Judging by the harsh expression on his face, he was simply looking for an excuse to use that wretched tape against her.

As she glanced away, defeated, he released her arm and, with one hand on her waist, propelled her towards the dining-room. 'Look, your friends are waiting,' he observed amusedly, nodding towards the two young Americans, who were hovering now uncertainly outside the dining-room door. 'You'd better go and tell them you've changed your plans.' He gave her a sharp push in their direction. 'Kindly be as quick as you can. I'll be waiting for you at our table.'

On legs that were rigid with indignation, Olinda did as she was bade. If she had hated him before, she loathed him now for this calculated humiliation. You bastard, Guy de Chevalley, she was swearing to herself. I'll find a way to make you eat dirt if it's the very last thing I ever do!

CHAPTER THREE

OVER the next couple of days Guy played Olinda like an expert fisherman played a fish on a line.

From time to time the line would slacken and she would find herself free to come and go as she pleased without feeling his eyes watching her every move. But then, just as she was starting to enjoy this freedom, with a masterful jerk he would draw the line in. Like the unprincipled sadist that he was, he seemed to be thoroughly enjoying the hold he had over her.

But at least, as yet, the only really serious imposition he had made on her had been to demand her presence at his table at mealtimes—mealtimes which she had doggedly ensured were sullen, silent and exceedingly brief. There had, fortunately, been no further allusions to blackmail.

All the same, her stay in Miami had been ruined. The conference had been both thought-provoking and informative, but any real enjoyment she might have derived from it had been thoroughly blighted by Guy's hovering dark presence. She was glad when at last the final day arrived and she could look forward to leaving him behind her for good. Before her stretched two weeks in Barbados. At least he wouldn't be around to spoil that!

Oddly, however, there was no sign of Guy at lunch-time that final day. Olinda had seen him in the lecture hall earlier, but he failed to join the other conference-goers when everyone adjourned for lunch. Olinda ate alone at their customary table, congratulating herself on this piece of good luck. And, for the first time for days, she could actually enjoy what she was eating, instead of bolting it down like a hungry dog!

She had even more reason for quiet celebration when she went down for dinner just before eight. She had known it was to be a special evening—a dance band had been hired for the occasion and everyone had been requested to wear formal dress. As she had got dressed in her room in her favourite pink two-piece, her soft brown hair tied up in a topknot, she had secretly rather been resenting the prospect that Guy was destined to spoil this evening as well.

But as eight o'clock, and then eight-thirty, came and went and there was still no sign of him, Olinda started to feel her spirits lift. Perhaps he had already left Miami. Perhaps some crisis had forced his return to France.

She crossed her fingers. That would indeed be a blessing. It would mean that she was unlikely ever to set eyes on him again. And, more immediately, it would also mean that she was free to enjoy herself tonight.

Right on cue, at that very moment, a shadow appeared silently at her side.

'Since you're on your own,' a friendly voice was saying, 'I thought you might like to join me and Gerry?'

Olinda glanced up to find Elliot standing there, smiling down at her with warm brown eyes. She didn't hesitate. 'I'd absolutely love to.' Then she gathered up her bag and allowed him to escort her across the room.

Since that unfortunate incident two days ago when

Guy had obliged her, in such humiliating fashion, to renege on her plans to have lunch with them, Olinda had continued to be friendly with the two young Americans, even managing to join them for the occasional lecture.

She had explained away her association with Guy by saying he was an acquaintance of her boss. 'I'm expected to be nice to him,' she'd lied, not bothering to explain why she found that such a chore, 'so I'm really obliged to share his table.'

Neither Elliot nor Gerry were the type to ask questions, so they had accepted her explanation and said no more, but Olinda nevertheless had not forgiven Guy for the utter fool he had made of her that day.

Still, all that was behind her now, she told herself with a secret smile of triumph, as she settled down at her young friends' table to enjoy the evening ahead.

'So you're off to Barbados,' Gerry was saying. 'I sure wish I was coming with you.'

Elliot smiled across at her. 'Skip Barbados. Come and spend a couple of weeks in Philadelphia instead.'

Olinda laughed. 'I'd love to see Philadelphia, and the rest of the United States, come to that. But there's no way you're going to talk me out of Barbados. This is the dream holiday I never thought I'd have.'

Elliot shook his head. 'Well, at least I tried.' Then he added, deliberately holding her eyes, 'Seriously, though, if you ever come back to the States, look me up. I'd love to show you around.'

Olinda smiled back at him. Elliot was nice. In other circumstances she would have liked to get to know him better. He was the kind of boy she had always wished she could fall in love with, a million light years away from types like Julian. But, although she had had several short romances with boys like Elliot over the past three years since her heartbreak with Julian, they were romances that, somehow, had never developed. Instead of becoming lovers, the boys had ended up as friends.

She sighed to herself. In matters of love the Steven women had no luck at all. Her mother had married a hopeless ne'er-do-well who had left her in the lurch with two small daughters, and then look at what had happened to Dolores. Her own experience with Julian had been minor in comparison—he had at least had the decency to betray her before she had become physically involved with him—but the experience had taught her a salutary lesson.

She might, like her mother and her sister, have a propensity to fall for the wrong sort of man, but she was determined that, unlike them, she would end up as no man's victim. Rather than that, she would sacrifice love and settle for liking and respect in its place. And liking and respect were precisely the emotions she knew that she could feel for Elliot.

She smiled across at him now. 'If I'm ever over in the States again, I'll remember your offer,' she promised.

'Good girl! I mean it.' Then he touched her arm. 'How about a dance?'

Without a moment's hesitation, Olinda rose to her feet. 'I'd love to,' she assured him.

His arms about her were soft and gentle as he guided her across the floor, and as they danced Olinda hummed softly beneath her breath the familiar tune that the band was playing. For virtually the first time in these stressful three days she felt relaxed and untroubled, at peace with herself.

A moment later her tranquillity was shattered with the ferocity of a firecracker blowing up in her face.

As though inexorably drawn by some magnetic power, her eyes had strayed across the room to the table where she had begun the evening. And a jolt like an electric current went through her at the sight of the lone dark figure seated there.

A chill went through her. So he was back. He had not returned to France, after all. Feeling suddenly sick, for she knew he had seen her—the blue eyes had driven right through her like skewers—Olinda snatched her gaze away and, involuntarily, she drew a little closer to Elliot, letting her jaw rest lightly on his shoulder, as the hostile blue eyes continued to pursue her, as deadly as rattlesnakes, across the room.

She felt Elliot's arms tighten. 'Are you enjoying yourself?'

She nodded without thinking. 'Mmm. Yes,' she supplied.

But her mind was not on dancing any more, but filled with a sudden dark sense of dread. Why had Guy come back now, when the conference was already finished? And why was he watching her in that deadly fashion, like an eagle about to swoop on its prey?

She did not have long to wait for her answer.

'Excuse me. May I have the pleasure?'

All at once, the tall, dark-suited figure of Guy de Chevalley had materialised at Elliot's right shoulder.

As he smiled, the harsh lines vanished from his features, and the blue eyes radiated a deadly charm as they flicked from Elliot to Olinda, then back to Elliot once again.

He repeated his request—'May I have the pleasure?'—in a tone that precluded a negative response. And, even before Elliot started to relinquish her, one sun-browned hand was already reaching out to take eloquent possession of Olinda's arm.

But in spite of the apprehension that clenched inside her Olinda was not so easily overawed as her partner. 'Hey, wait a minute!' she started to protest, her heart sinking abruptly into her stomach as Elliot let his hand drop away from her waist and Guy de Chevalley took masterful charge. 'What the hell do you think you're playing at?'

One black eyebrow arced in response. 'What does it look like? I'm cutting in.'

'It's all right, Olinda. You go ahead.' With a thin smile Elliot sought to placate her, as, with a shrug, he retreated to watch from the sidelines.

'You see?' purred Guy de Chevalley, smiling down at her wickedly. 'Your partner doesn't mind in the least.'

'Well, I do!' she seethed back at him in fury. 'Kindly let me go this minute!'

'Not a chance.' His smile never wavered, though some of the charm had vanished from his eyes. 'You're going to dance this dance with me, *chérie*, whether you happen to like it or not.' Lest she harbour any inclination that he might be joking, his already firm grasp around her tightened. 'So why not just relax and try to look as though you're enjoying it?'

Olinda glared at him. 'Don't ask the impossible!' Her soft mouth set in a belligerent line. 'Maybe you can force me to dance with you, but there's no way you can make me pretend to enjoy it!'

'Suit yourself.' He shrugged his indifference, as his arm drew her taut body more closely against him. 'I confess I also would prefer a more congenial partner, but one must learn to take one's pleasures where one finds them.'

Unprincipled bastard! Olinda scowled at him. Did he possess no shame as well as no scruples? And she gritted her teeth and glared straight ahead of her as, with elegant grace, he swept her round the floor.

But it was hard to keep the scowl fixed on her face and her mind focused firmly on her anger and outrage, for the strangest things were suddenly happening to her senses.

Hot needles of awareness were coursing through her veins as the hand at her back pressed warmly against her, the firm, hard fingers that held her prisoner sending currents of electricity rippling up and down her spine. And the way her breasts were crushed against him, so that she could feel the rise and fall of his chest, was sending tiny palpitations through her heart.

It was quite inexplicable, she found herself arguing, that every brush of his thigh should set her pulses racing, and it was a downright disgrace that the nearness of his jaw that now and then lightly touched her temple was making her tongue stick like sawdust to the roof of her mouth. And yet she could not deny that it was happening, nor that, in spite of her resistance, these sensations were pleasurable.

Little wonder, she thought dully, that poor Dolores had fallen so helplessly under his spell. She, after all, had been subjected to an onslaught of considerably more fervour and intimacy than this!

At the thought a strange sensation drove through her and settled, lambent, in the pit of her stomach. What must it be like, she found herself wondering, to share that total, ultimate intimacy with so potent and vibrantly sexual a man?

The question shamed her, even as it came to her, but she could not stop it from uncurling like a serpent in her mind. And, for one cravenly ridiculous instant, she almost felt envious of her sister. Dolores had dared to taste these wild pleasures, something she herself would never dare to do. Call it cowardice or common sense, but she would run a million miles before she would ever dare to surrender to a man as dangerous as Guy de Chevalley.

'You missed my company for lunch today?' Suddenly she realised he had spoken, jerking her from her shameful reverie.

Olinda forced herself to look at him, struggling for detachment. 'I missed you,' she said flatly, 'like a dose of the plague.'

But Guy merely smiled. 'I love your British humour. It's so refreshing and so very subtle.' He let his eyes sweep amusedly over her face, his wide mouth quirking sensuously at the corners. Then his expression seemed abruptly to harden. 'But I think I have had enough of humour for the moment, and also enough of dancing. I suggest we adjourn to somewhere more private.' He paused and fixed her with his dark cobalt gaze. 'To your room, *chérie*, to be more precise.'

Olinda stiffened. 'I beg your pardon? I don't think I understood correctly.'

Guy smiled again. 'More British subtlety?' Then, with a blatant sensuality that was neither British nor subtle, he deliberately let his fingers trail up through her hair, sending the wildest sensation skittering across her scalp. 'Don't worry, *ma belle*, you will understand everything just as soon as you and I are alone.'

Olinda was liking the prospect less and less. Affecting innocence, she demanded huskily, 'Need we really be alone? Whatever it is, couldn't we deal with it here?'

He shook his dark head. 'Come, come, *chérie*. Where is your British love of privacy?' Then his fingers tightened around her arm, dissuading her from further argument. 'Just as soon as the music ends, you will go and make your excuses to your boyfriends. Then return immediately to your room and wait for me—*alone*,' he stressed. 'I will come to you in half an hour's time. Be sure to do as I say!'

At that very moment the music stopped, and with a final dark glance Guy turned and left her to find her own way back to her table. As she approached, Elliot rose politely to his feet, a look of mild concern on his face.

'Are you OK, Olinda?' he queried, frowning. 'You suddenly look a little pale.'

Thank you, Elliot. It was a perfect opening. 'Yes, I do feel a bit peculiar,' she agreed. 'It came over me quite suddenly.' She sighed and ran a limp hand over her brow and glanced down to include Gerry as she carried on, 'Would you mind terribly if I went up to my room? I think I need to lie down for a bit.'

'Of course not. I'll come with you.' Already Elliot was moving towards her. 'Come on, take my arm. You really don't look well at all.'

'That's really not necessary. I'll manage,' she protested. But Elliot, for once, was adamant.

'I'm coming with you,' he insisted. 'So just say goodnight to Gerry and we'll be on our way.'

There was no point in making a fuss, Olinda decided, as she shook hands with Gerry and took Elliot's arm. The situation was already quite embarrassing enough. And as she and her young escort made their journey out into the lobby, Olinda couldn't help wondering if Guy was watching, and maybe even cynically applauding her performance. And she cursed him quietly to herself for bringing this second humiliation down on her—though somehow she suspected that her present discomfort was nothing compared to what lay ahead.

She kept the final farewells with Elliot brief.

As she fumbled with her room key, he offered kindly, 'Shall I get the hotel to send you up some aspirins, or maybe a hot drink, if you'd like that? I could even contact the hotel doctor, if you like?'

Olinda shook her head. Heaven forbid! 'No, thanks. I'll be all right. I think all I need is a good night's rest.'

'OK, if you insist.' Then he frowned as she pushed open the door. 'I'm sorry I won't be able to see you again before I leave. As you know, my flight back to Philadelphia's at the crack of dawn tomorrow.' Soft brown eyes looked into her face. 'However, I hope you

enjoy your holiday in Barbados. And remember my
offer—I was serious. If you're ever over in the States
again, be sure to look me up. You have my address.'

She smiled back at him warmly. 'It's unlikely, but if I
am I'll get in touch.' She held out her hand to him.
'Goodbye, Elliot. I hope you have a good flight back.'

Then she was utterly and totally taken aback as he
leaned very quickly and kissed her on the cheek. He
squeezed her hand. 'Have a good night's sleep. I hope
you feel better in the morning.'

Once in her room, as she closed the door behind her,
Olinda couldn't suppress a smile. She had been right
about Elliot, he was a really nice guy, the kind she
always hit it off easily with. It really was a shame and a
waste that she had been denied the chance to get to
know him better.

She kicked off her shoes and crossed to the fridge bar
to get herself a can of orange juice. She had that
wrecker de Chevalley to thank for that—just one of a
growing list of bad turns he had done her. She poured
the orange juice into a glass and stole a quick glance at
her watch, just as a sharp tap sounded on the door.

With a twang of apprehension she hurried to answer
it. 'You're early!' she snapped, as Guy strode into the
room.

In typical fashion, he ignored her protest and made
himself comfortable in one of the armchairs. 'That was
quite a touching little scene out there with the boyfriend. Sorry if this appointment of ours cramped your
style.'

How dared he? She glared at him. 'I had no idea you

were a Peeping Tom—on top of all your other attributes! But I suppose I should have known no pastime is too low for you!'

He leaned back a little and smiled a wicked smile, not in the slightest put out by her attack. 'Don't flatter yourself, I wasn't peeping. I just happened to come round the corner at a particularly poignant moment. But I promise I made a strategic withdrawal until I was sure the moment was over.'

Olinda turned away from him, privately seething, and retrieved her orange juice from the fridge top where she had left it. He was being despicable as usual, despoiling with his lewd, irreverent sense of humour a warm and perfectly innocent friendship.

Wearing a look of disdain, she turned round to face him. 'You said downstairs that you had something to tell me.' She lowered herself with composure on to a nearby chair and took a mouthful of her drink. 'Perhaps now you would be good enough to get on and tell me.'

He raised devil's wing eyebrows and queried smoothly, 'Did I say that—that I had something to tell you? I seem simply to remember saying that I wished to see you privately.'

He was right, he had. Olinda squirmed inwardly, as mocking blue eyes continued to watch her. Though it was not his mockery that particularly disturbed her, more the sensuous curve of his wide, well-shaped mouth. Alone here in this room with him, and knowing that she was at his mercy, she felt the raw sexuality he radiated unsettling in the extreme.

Guy paused a moment, evidently relishing her discomfort, and stretched his long legs out in front of him.

'As a matter of fact,' he put to her finally, 'I wish to make you a proposition.' Then, as she visibly tensed, he reached inside his jacket and pulled out a folded piece of newsprint. He unfolded it carefully and held it out to her. 'But first, I think you should have a look at this.'

It was an article cut from a local newspaper. What, at a quick glance, looked like the gossip column, and entitled 'Love Among the Eggheads'. And though her eyes needed a moment to focus on the small print, what needed little deciphering was the picture in one corner.

'It's you and me!' Olinda stammered, aghast. 'Someone must have taken it here in the hotel. It's you and me having dinner at your table.' Though the gross misrepresentation it portrayed literally took her breath away. Somehow, in the picture she and Guy de Chevalley appeared to be gazing soulfully into one another's eyes. She swallowed miserably. It was there in black and white. Who said the camera never lied?

'The picture's the least of it. Wait till you read the story.' Guy flicked the cutting from her suddenly frozen fingers and saved her the trouble by reading aloud an excerpt. '"Millionaire French playboy Guy de Chevalley, currently in Miami for the international science conference, has been taking time out from more weighty matters to spend romantic evenings with his latest *amour*, pretty brunette Olinda Steven, from Surrey in England". . .'

As he broke off and glanced across at her, Olinda felt her blood grow cold. This was the same sort of stuff she had read about him in various newspapers over the years. In the past, she had simply shaken her head disapprovingly and turned over to another page. But this was outrageous! Sheer invention! How could anyone have the bad taste to print such a vile, fictitious story about *her*?

Guy was watching her. 'Would you like to hear more? There are a couple more paragraphs in the same vein.'

Olinda's mouth had thinned to a straight line. 'No, I do not want to hear more!' she assured him emphatically. 'What I want is for something to be done about it! I demand that you get in touch with the editor of the paper and order him to retract this story immediately!'

Guy smiled. 'You flatter me, *ma chère*, that you should assume I possess such power.' Then he straightened a little, pushing back the sides of the elegantly immaculate black jacket he was wearing. 'However, by a strange coincidence, I did in fact spend most of this afternoon at the *Bugle*, talking to the editor in question.'

So that was where he had been! Olinda watched him closely, as he carefully loosened the silk tie at his throat. 'Weren't you able to persuade him to print a retraction?'

Guy shook his head. 'I didn't even try. This sort of nonsense, though irritating, is harmless.' With a contemptuous gesture he crumpled the piece of paper and tossed it, with uncanny accuracy, into the waste bin in the corner. 'It isn't worth getting upset about.'

That was easy enough for him to say! 'You may not think so, but I'm afraid I do! We all know how *you* love drawing Press attention to yourself, but I'm not used to having things printed about me in the gossip columns!'

Guy threw her a hard look. 'Is that so, *chérie*? Well, perhaps you'd better start getting used to it!'

Olinda recoiled at the threat in his voice. 'And what is that supposed to mean?'

He kept his eyes fixed on her, their expression flat and dangerous, as, with studied contempt, he ignored her question and reached once more into his inside pocket to draw out another piece of paper. He held it up between them. 'This is the reason I went to speak to the *Bugle*'s editor, Ed Krech, today. It's the letter that accompanied the cutting—delivered by hand to the hotel this morning, and anonymous, needless to say.'

As he made no attempt to hand it over to her, Olinda enquired curiously, 'And what does it say?'

Guy refolded the piece of paper, returned it to his pocket and ran long, tanned fingers over his dark hair. 'I have no idea who sent it—it wasn't anyone on the paper—but it's a warning, *chérie*, that my enemies are out to get me and that they will use every means possible to blacken my name.'

Olinda continued to regard him levelly. It did not surprise her in the slightest to discover that Guy de Chevalley had enemies. 'I would have thought their task would be infinitely easy,' she observed without a flicker of sympathy. 'A man like yourself——' she paused censoriously '—must have much in his past of which he is ashamed.'

Guy smiled a brittly cynical smile. 'That appears to be their conclusion too. They are at pains to inform me that, in addition to the spies they currently have watching me night and day, they are also employing a number of experts to dig into my murky past.'

An unenviable task, Olinda decided. Rather like wading through an open sewer. She took a clean, cool mouthful of orange juice. 'And what is the purpose behind all this?' she questioned. 'I assume they're not simply indulging in such a pastime out of some perverted taste for voyeurism?'

'Indeed not.' He leaned back easily in his chair and hooked one ankle over the opposite thigh. 'Their plan, apparently, is to try and stop me taking over a local drugs company which I'm currently in the process of negotiating for. It happens to be a particularly important takeover. The very future of the Foundation could be affected if it should fail to proceed as planned—a fact which the anonymous author of that letter appears to be all too well aware of.

'That's the reason I'm over here, by the way. In order to handle the negotiations personally. As you so rightly pointed out at our first meeting, I rarely have time to attend these conferences.'

He sighed and ran one finger down his well-shaped nose. 'As always when one is involved in takeovers, there has been some local opposition, fairly vociferous at times. My anonymous correspondent seems to believe that it is within his power to unearth some scurrilous piece of gossip about me that will finally swing the balance against me.'

And the best of luck to him, Olinda thought maliciously. Whoever he was, if it was his aim to topple the execrable Guy de Chevalley, he had her full and wholehearted support. The only thing that bothered her in all of this was that she had somehow become involved.

She straightened in her seat. 'So what was the purpose of that article in today's paper? As you said yourself, it's pretty tame stuff. They're surely going to need something a lot stronger than that?'

Guy shrugged his broad shoulders. 'Oh, that was just a taster. Just to convince me that they really are watching me and that the paper is prepared to print stories about me. The paper in question happens to be one that has more or less led the campaign against the takeover. They'd be more than happy to publish all the dirt they could lay hands on—which is why I took it upon myself to go and confront Krech today. I wanted him to tell me who's feeding him the story.'

Olinda leaned forward. 'And did he?' she asked.

'No chance. As I expected, he insisted that he could not reveal his sources—so I made a point of laying a very serious warning on him that I would sue his paper to kingdom come if he printed anything damaging about me.'

At the dark ferocity that suddenly flooded his features, a shiver, like cold fingers, trickled down her spine. Guy de Chevalley would make an uncomfortable enemy. Ruthless, cruel and unforgiving. Olinda kept quiet as he continued,

'I also paid a call to the local police chief, just to put him in the picture, and I've hired myself a private detective to try and track down who's behind the whole thing.'

It was beginning to sound like a gangster movie! Private detectives and police chiefs, no less! 'It sounds as if you've got the whole thing sewn up, then,' she observed in a tone of mild regret. 'It seems unlikely they'll be able to do you any damage now.'

'Possibly you're right. It does seem unlikely—but there's no way I'm going to let the matter rest there. I'm personally going to get whoever's behind this and teach them a lesson they'll never forget.' A look like thunder darkened his face. 'No one sends anonymous threats to me and gets away with it,' he ground.

Olinda observed his tautened features and the eyes that burned like liquid blue fire. 'You've got the private detective dealing with that. Surely it's just a matter of time?'

He hissed with impatience through his teeth. 'Time, at this stage, is something I'm short of. The negotiations are now over and a local committee are due to make up their minds about the takeover within the month.' He stood up abruptly, clenching his fists. 'That's why I have to do something myself. The private detective was just a back-up, a kind of safety net, in case I fail.' He swung round suddenly to face her. 'But I won't fail—if I have you to help me.'

Olinda blinked, openly staggered at the suggestion. Why, she was inwardly cheering on his enemies, not looking for a way to help him out of his mess! She threw him a look of purest grey granite. 'And why should I help you?' she challenged.

It was a stupid question, as he instantly demonstrated. 'There is the small question of a tape,' he reminded her sharply.

That damnable tape! How could she have forgotten? 'You mean if I don't——?' She broke off, appalled, as the awful possibilities all at once crowded in on her.

Guy smiled sadistically. 'That's precisely what I mean. Should you be so unwise as to refuse to co-operate, I shall make a formal complaint against you to the conference organisers, as well, quite naturally, as supplying your employers with copies of the tape.'

Olinda fumbled to defend herself. 'It's too late! It won't work now! You've waited too long! Why would you have sought my company every mealtime if you suspected I was some kind of spy?'

Guy parried smoothly, 'That's easily explained. It was you, *ma chère*, who sought my company. I went along with you in the hope that you would confess to me privately what you were up to. I had hoped, you see, that I might avoid having to expose you—you seemed on the surface such a nice, wholesome girl. But alas. . .' he mimicked a look of regret, '. . .in the end, you more or less forced my hand. You really left me with no choice.'

Olinda felt the cold hand of defeat upon her. As her sister, too, had discovered to her cost, he was a colourful and consummate liar. If he really wanted to, he would make his story stick. For even if she were to reveal now who she was and try to use his involvement with Dolores against him, the attempt would only backfire in her face. It would simply look as though she had been out to repay him by indulging in a spot of industrial espionage.

She looked back at him dully, as he told her, 'You see what I mean? You haven't a hope. I really think you would be wise to co-operate.'

Olinda clenched her teeth until her jaw hurt. She could scarcely have been faced with a more appalling prospect. But suddenly the threat of losing that pro-motion—or, even worse, she feared now, her job itself—seemed like a terrifyingly real possibility. This man, she knew, would stop at nothing.

She looked up into his face with a sincere and heartfelt loathing. 'What do you want me to do?' she mumbled.

'That's more like it.' His dark expression softened. 'I'm glad I've been able to make you see sense.' He slid his hands into his trouser pockets and slowly circled the chair where she sat. 'What I want you to do is very simple and will require only the smallest rearrangement of your plans. . .'

As he paused before her, she could feel her heart thumping with the tension of waiting for what was coming next. But a moment later it stopped beating altogether, as, in the cool tones of one proposing a harmless game of ludo, he informed her, 'You, *chérie*, have a treat in store.' He sat down on his seat again and leaned towards her. 'You and I are about to have a passionate affair.'

CHAPTER FOUR

THE glass of orange juice she was holding very nearly dropped from Olinda's hand. Her eyes snapped open like umbrellas. '*What* did you say?' she stuttered in horror.

'What's the matter? Don't you care for the idea?' Guy grinned at her, an almost impish grin, his wide mouth dimpling wickedly at the corners. 'There are many women, I assure you, who would jump at the chance of an affair with Guy de Chevalley.'

Such bare-faced vanity! 'So let them jump! But I'm sorry to disappoint you! I'm not one of them! And I think you have an unspeakable nerve even to consider making such a suggestion!'

In the face of this display of righteous indignation the smile on his face had simply grown wider. In addition to having no discernible taste, the man evidently possessed a groteque sense of humour!

Olinda watched him warily from her seat as he drew his own seat a little closer. 'Calm down, *chérie*. You take me too literally. The affair I had in mind was not a real one, simply a façade for the benefit of our public.'

And what was that supposed to mean? She shook her head and continued to scowl at him. 'I'm sorry, I'm afraid I don't understand.'

'Then let me explain.' He leaned back in his seat and touched his hands together, making a steeple with his long, tanned fingers. Then he leaned his dark chin lightly on its apex and regarded her from beneath long, sooty lashes. 'As I told you a moment ago, it is my intention to catch whoever it is who's behind this attempt to sabotage the takeover. No doubt I could manage it on my own, but I have decided it might be quicker if I enlist your assistance.'

'Enlist, you call it? You almost make it sound voluntary!'

'Come, come, *chérie*. Let us not quibble over details.' He dismissed her sarcasm with a wave of one hand and continued his explanations where he had left off. 'What I intend to do is cash in on the interest that our relationship appears to have aroused. The spies who are watching us believe that we are engaged in some sort of torrid love affair. . .' He broke off with a smile of satanic enjoyment to observe the harsh distaste on her face. '. . .So what could be more natural for two lovers like ourselves than that we should take ourselves off for a romantic little sojourn on an idyllic sun-drenched Caribbean island?

'Naturally, our spies will follow us, believing us to be too wrapped up in each other to pay much attention to what they're up to. It shouldn't take too much ingenuity on our part to trick them into revealing who they are.'

As he paused, apparently awaiting her reaction, Olinda laid down the glass of orange juice she was still holding and regarded him with hostile grey eyes. What was all this talk of 'we' and 'us'? He was assuming, even before he had properly put his plan to her, that she had agreed to go along with it. But she did not voice the observation, for she knew how he would answer her. He would simply remind her about the tape. So, instead, she proceeded to pick holes in his logic.

'Surely, after the threats they've made, they would be expecting you to be very much on your guard? In fact, if you ask me, they would immediately suspect that it's a set-up.'

Guy smiled at her. 'Nice try,' he acknowledged. 'But psychology, I can see, is not your strong point. Far from believing it was a set-up, they would simply assume that I was behaving in character. It would not be the first time in my life that I have taken time out with an attractive young lady.'

Indeed not. As he paused for a moment to underline the point with the provocative lifting of one jet-black eyebrow, Olinda could see that her attempt at rebuttal was about to be systematically demolished. He did not disappoint her, as he continued,

'Anyone who professes to know me—and these enemies of mine are not strangers, I am sure of it— knows that I am not the type instantly to collapse in the face of some threat. They know I will not easily alter my lifestyle—I'm sure they would be suspicious if I did. In fact they know it would be a point of honour with me to treat their threats with the contempt they deserve.'

Olinda could scarcely argue with that, as she suppressed a wry and faintly surprised smile at this rare and unexpected display of self-knowledge. At least he was capable of being honest about himself. He admitted he was nothing but an arrogant womaniser who put his own selfish whims and desires above all.

She chose, however, to ignore his next remark, which he spoke in a low voice, almost as an aside.

'Naturally, they will believe all these things because they choose to believe all the nonsense they read.'

Nonsense, my eye! She regarded him cynically, as a sudden sharp image of Dolores crossed her mind. Unfortunately for Guy, she had personal knowledge of just how accurate that so-called nonsense really was.

She narrowed her eyes and made another stab at arguing her way out of this trap he was weaving. 'Why don't you just go to this committee you mentioned—the one that has to decide about the takeover—and explain to them what's going on? You could warn them in advance not to believe any damaging stories that might appear about you in the Press.'

'And plant doubts in their minds about my integrity? No, *chérie*.' He shook his dark head. 'Professional suicide is not in my repertoire. And anyway——' he pulled a shrug '—even if I were to convince the committee, such stories would turn the public against me and I would find myself once more back where I started.'

'Get a court injunction against the paper.' She smiled as this brainwave popped into her head. 'Have them stopped from publishing any damaging material.'

Guy smiled. 'Your attempts to assist me are really most touching. However, I'm afraid that suggestion would not work, either. Even if I succeeded in getting an injunction, my enemies could simply approach another paper. I can hardly,' he argued with unimpeachable logic, 'seek injunctions against every newspaper in the world.'

Olinda felt herself sag. She was getting nowhere. For every smart argument she came up with he had an even smarter answer. 'Well, I don't see why you personally have to do anything anyway,' she shot back with a sudden flash of irritation. 'You told me you've hired a private detective, so why can't you just leave it to him?'

'I may have to in the end.' He regarded her obliquely. 'But as I told you before, the private detective is just a back-up. I would prefer to solve this mystery myself.'

'You prefer to buy a dog and then bark yourself!' He was being infuriatingly stubborn!

Guy laughed at the analogy. 'If you say so. But I'm hoping to do a great deal more than just bark. As a matter of fact I'm rather looking forward to the pleasure of sinking my teeth into their guilty hides.' He smiled ferociously. 'This is no game. It is a personal challenge which I do not intend shirking.'

Olinda grimaced. She had her answer. All the most sophisticated and logical arguments she could muster, she now knew, would be a total waste of time. He was going to all this trouble and subterfuge—into which he was also intending to drag her—for the primitive macho pleasure of hand-to-hand combat. It was not enough that his tormentors be brought to book. He personally had to have the pleasure of dealing the final bloody blow!

Damn him, she thought, and damn his male ego. 'Well, I'm not going to co-operate!' she exploded. 'It's just not necessary and I won't do it!'

'Oh, no, *chérie*?' Suddenly, without warning, he was leaning towards her, grasping the arms of her chair firmly in his hands, then, before she could do a thing to stop him, he was snatching the chair bodily towards him.

As their knees collided, Olinda let out a gasp, feeling a spasm of electricity go shafting through her. Then, as his hard thighs continued to press against hers, as he held her in the rigid prison of his arms, she was aware that her heart was pounding erratically, like a wild, frantic creature, straining for release. She could almost feel it hammering against her ribcage. The force of its beating froze the breath in her throat.

He thrust his face into hers, making her jerk away from him. 'I find it extremely tedious that I have to keep reminding you of what the situation between us is.' He gave the chair a shake, making her bones rattle. 'Is your memory really so defective, *chérie*?'

There was nothing in the slightest wrong with her memory. It was her voice at that moment that seemed suddenly to have deserted her. She opened her mouth to make some mutinous protest, but all that came out was an incoherent squeak.

'Surely you do not wish to force me into the position of having to expose you?' he gritted. 'That, for both of us, would be such a terrible waste.'

Olinda shook her head. Insincere bastard! 'I just can't agree to what you're proposing.'

'Why not?' The black brows knitted darkly. 'Is there some impediment that you have not told me about?' A sudden consideration seemed to flash into his mind. 'That young American friend of yours, for example. . . Is he planning to tag along with you to Barbados?'

For one desperate second she was tempted to say yes. The lie would be worth it, if it would even temporarily thwart him. But she knew all too well that it would make no difference, and that it would have made no difference even if it were true. A man like Guy de Chevalley did not allow the Elliots of this world to stand in his way. He simply pushed them aside or trampled all over them, just as he had done to Dolores.

She shook her head sullenly. 'No,' she confirmed. 'Elliot's not coming with me.'

'Well, then, *chérie*. . .' He shook her again. 'That's one less problem we have to deal with.' The dark blue eyes glittered into hers. 'Are there any other problems you have omitted to tell me about?'

Only that I hate and despise you, she thought, with every fibre of my being. And that I will never forgive you for what you did to Dolores and that I pray you rot in hell forever!

But he was waiting for her answer. 'If there are no other problems, I assume I can take it that you will, after all, co-operate?'

Olinda looked into his face, on the brink of defeat, hating herself for the way she had tied this noose around her neck. How would she ever live with herself now, knowing that she, his most bitter enemy, had been manipulated into acting as an ally? It was not his salvation she should be embarked on, rather his annihilation.

And then it came to her. A bolt from the blue. Suddenly, the very thing that she had been praying for was staring her straight in the face!

With an effort she fought back her sudden elation and in a show of submission lowered her head. 'I have no choice,' she mumbled defeatedly. 'I'll do anything you say.'

But as, at last, he released her and rose from his chair, nodding his satisfaction at this timely capitulation, Olinda's heart was secretly soaring.

For suddenly it had come to her like a divine revelation. Suddenly she knew exactly how she could take her revenge!

Olinda could scarcely wait for morning to come.

For most of the night she lay in bed, plotting, her mind shimmering with the excitement of what she was planning. It was such an obvious move. She smiled in the darkness. How come it had taken her so long to think of it?

Still, better late than never, she acknowledged, as, for what must have been the thousandth time, she squinted at the luminous dial of her watch. But she didn't really care if she slept or not. There was too much to think of, too much to work out. For the task ahead was fraught with danger. Heaven protect her, she thought with a shiver, if Guy de Chevalley should ever find out.

She was up early next morning, and showered and dressed long before her usual time. Suddenly deeply grateful that she had set the precedent, she had breakfast in her room as usual, knocking back endless cups of black coffee, though too nervous to do justice to the waffles for once. Guy had ordered her to meet him in the lobby at nine-thirty, her cases packed and ready for the flight to Barbados. That meant that her time was extremely limited. She must make her move between nine and nine-thirty.

The instant the hands of her watch hit nine o'clock, she picked up the receiver of the phone by her bedside and punched in the numbers she had spent the night rehearsing. The number rang once and then there was a click.

'*Bugle* editorial,' a voice drawled into her ear.

Olinda's heart clenched with nervous excitement. She swallowed quickly to relieve her dry throat. 'I want to speak to the editor, Ed Krech,' she said firmly.

'I'm afraid Mr Krech isn't in his office yet. Would you like to leave a message, caller?'

Olinda gave a low moan of disappointment. This was the very thing she'd feared. 'No, I have to speak to him personally,' she answered. 'What time are you expecting him?'

'A little after ten or thereabouts. Can I get him to call you when he comes in?'

At ten or thereabouts she would be on her way to the airport and from there she would be leaving directly for Barbados. She felt a sudden stab of panic. Was she about to be thwarted for the sake of half an hour? 'No, that's no good.' Her brain was whirring. 'Perhaps there's someone eles I could talk to? What about the woman who writes the gossip column?'

'Miss Aurora Benjamin? She's not here either. But she's usually in the office around half-nine.'

Olinda felt like weeping with frustration. Every way she turned she met a brick wall. 'Just in case she comes in early, can you leave her a message and ask her to call me immediately? It really is incredibly urgent. I'll only be at this number for the next half-hour.'

The woman took a note of her name and number and

Olinda hung up, her insides in turmoil. She only had twenty-five minutes left. If this Benjamin woman didn't call back by then, she would have to abandon her entire plan.

She was pacing the room like a cat on hot cinders when the telephone rang, making her jump. She dived across the bed and grabbed the receiver. 'Hello? Olinda Steven here,' she gulped.

'Good morning, *chérie*.'

Olinda's heart sank like a lead balloon and her breath caught guiltily at the back of her throat.

'I'm just calling to remind you,' he continued, 'that we're meeting downstairs in twenty minutes' time.'

'I hadn't forgotten.' Her tone was terse. 'Don't worry, I'll be there. Goodbye.' She hung up.

By now she was almost on the point of screaming, her poor nerves stretched as taut as piano wire. She should have known this scheme of hers would come to nothing. Guy de Chevalley led a charmed life. It was a waste of time her trying to harm him.

She stared miserably at her watch. Thirteen minutes past. It felt like counting the minutes to one's own execution. She glanced at her reflection in the mirror. Nice try, Olinda. Too bad it failed.

And then, as all hope died within her, the phone burst shrilly into life. Hardly daring to hope, her heart frozen within her, Oinda reached for the receiver and pressed it to her ear. And a moment later she almost wept with happiness, as a female voice drawled, 'Aurora Benjamin here. I understand you wanted to speak to me?'

It took her just five minutes to say her piece. She had

rehearsed it endlessly. She was word-perfect. And it felt like a kind of exorcism to tell this unknown person on the end of the telephone all about Dolores and how Guy had killed her.

At the end of her expurgation there was a short pause. 'You realise we'll have to do some checking of our own before we can print this?' Miss Benjamin warned her.

'Check all you like. Every word of it is true. And as I told you, I intend winkling more secrets out of him—the sort of stuff I'm sure your paper would be interested in. You see,' Olinda added quickly, by way of explanation, 'I'm anxious to stop the takeover too.'

'I see.' The other woman seemed to consider her words thoughtfully. Then, 'I'm sure we would be very interested indeed to have a look at any stories you might come up with,' she agreed.

When Olinda once more laid down the receiver her hands were shaking uncontrollably, her stomach churning like a cement mixer, heavy with the sweet-sour wrath of revenge. I've done it! she congratulated herself weakly, her head swimming from the sheer enormity of her action. I've actually set the wheels in motion, the wheels that will ultimately carry Guy de Chevalley to his well-deserved and overdue ruin!

She only just had time to dash downstairs to reception to settle and then destroy the incriminating phone bill before hurtling along the corridor to the ladies' restroom and being violently and copiously sick.

'Relax, *chérie*. Try to smile a little. Remember, we're supposed to be two starry-eyed lovers embarking on a romantic Caribbean idyll.'

He had such a fanciful turn of phrase, Olinda was thinking irritably, as she sought, discreetly, to wriggle free from the arm that was draped too familiarly around her waist. They were climbing up the gangway of the plane that was to take them on their flight to Barbados—a name which now summoned up a rather different image from that of the sun-drenched, carefree paradise she had once dreamed of visiting. Espionage and danger were what now awaited her there.

And yet, she knew, she must disguise her apprehension and somehow smother the nagging sense of distaste that she innately felt for what she was doing. She was playing against a man who possessed no moral scruples. She had no choice but to play by his rules.

Rather than torture herself with destructive guilt and anxiety she would do better to concentrate on the task in hand, on how she could manage to strike a credible balance between the two opposing parts she now had to play. On the one hand she was Guy's reluctant companion, but at the same time she must worm her way into his confidence sufficiently to encourage him to open up to her.

It would be no easy task, for he was not an idiot. If she were to change her attitude to him too abruptly, he would, quite naturally, become suspicious. And yet it was essential that she act quickly. She had limited time and she must not waste this opportunity to gather as much evidence against him as possible. She would never have such a chance to get back at him again.

It was in this determined frame of mind that she had finally emerged from the rest-room to meet him in the lobby. And though she had outwardly flinched, she had inwardly smiled as he had bent to greet her with a false lover's kiss. The game had acquired a completely new flavour now that she had secretly altered its goals. Guy was blissfully unaware of it, but she was now using him as much as he was using her.

The flight from Miami to Barbados took just under four hours, during which time Olinda had the opportunity, for the first time in her life, to savour the delights of first-class travel.

'I always travel first class,' Guy had told her, tossing aside her own economy class ticket, as though it were a worthless scrap of paper. 'And so do the ladies who travel with me.' He had smiled complacently, knowing how much it grated on her to hear herself defined as one of his 'ladies'. 'And naturally,' he had elaborated silkily, 'I have made appropriate arrangements for our accommodation. When we arrive you can cancel the hotel you've booked. I shall pay whatever they deem you owe them.'

Amusement had flashed in his eyes, as he continued, 'I'm sure you'll be more comfortable where we're going. At least you can be certain there will be no cockroaches.' Then, 'Smile!' he had admonished her as she scowled back at him. 'Try to work a little harder to convince our public. If you insist on looking so down in the mouth they will be suspecting that you bear some grudge against me—that perhaps I did not make love to you often enough last night.'

He was shameless and hateful and quite without morality, just as she had always known he was. But at least, Olinda congratulated herself, as she turned to the crossword in the in-flight magazine, she was playing her dual role convincingly. So far he suspected nothing.

Then, at last, the plane was curving earthwards, and for a moment or two Olinda forgot her apprehension, as she leaned excitedly to peer out of the window. And at the sight that met her eyes she gasped with wonder.

Below stretched a huge expanse of sea, sapphire-blue and sparkling in the sun like some immense and priceless jewel, and in its midst a tiny emerald island, no bigger than a pocket handkerchief at first, but growing every larger and more breathtakingly beautiful as the plane continued to circle downwards. The magical island of Barbados. A Caribbean paradise.

She could make out the individual palm trees now, the higgledy-piggledy groups of multi-coloured houses and the endless beaches that circled the island like a shimmering pale silver ribbon.

'Beautiful, is it not?' Guy leaned to look past her. And Olinda nodded in agreement. This once, at least, she could not take issue with him. She had never seen anything more beautiful in her life.

The taxi ride from the airport was equally thrilling. Quite mesmerised by the lush, bright beauty of it all, Olinda's eyes darted from side to side, taking in the undulating, soft green hills, spiked with scarlet hibiscus and the clouds of glorious bougainvillaea, and the majestic, rolling Caribbean, every shade of blue it was possible to imagine.

She had expected the island to be exotic and beautiful, but the sheer exquisiteness of it took her breath away.

She was brought down to earth with a bump, however, as the taxi suddenly peeled off the highway.

Without warning, they were passing through a pair of tall gates that bore the legend 'Silver Cove'. It was the name she had heard Guy give to the taxi-driver, and she had assumed it to be the name of a hotel. But this was no hotel they were approaching now along a curving driveway lined with palm trees. The luxurious-looking building with its balconies and terraces was quite evidently a private villa.

With a stab of alarm, she turned to Guy. 'Where are you taking me?' she demanded to know.

He raised one dark eyebrow and smiled back at her innocently. 'What's the matter? Don't you like it?' he enquired.

Whether she liked it or not was hardly the issue— and there was no denying it was a fabulous-looking place. What mattered was that it was a private villa, miles away from anywhere. She glared at him through narrowed grey eyes. 'I assumed we'd be staying at a hotel.'

The wide lips dimpled at the corners as he returned her glare with a wicked smile. 'No, no, *chérie*, two lovers like ourselves require the utmost privacy—and here we shall be quite alone together. Surely you would not have wished the anonymity of a hotel, with the constant bother of people all around us?'

That was precisely what she would have wished—to be surrounded by the reassuring presence of others. But already they had come to a sweeping halt in the flower-festooned courtyard at the front of the house, and the taxi-driver was climbing out and coming round to open her door for her.

Olinda swore to herself. De Chevalley had tricked her. And she had been so busy feeling pleased with her own plans that it had never even crossed her mind to suspect. From now on she must learn to be more vigilant, or he was capable of even more devious moves than this.

The main door of the house was on the first floor, approached by a wooden staircase and circled by a veranda. As they approached the stairs, the door opened suddenly and a local woman, smiling broadly, hurried down to the courtyard to welcome them. 'I'm Marilyn,' she announced. 'The agency sent me to look after you.'

Thank goodness for that! With a sense of relief Olinda returned the woman's smile, taking in the homely figure, dressed in a red-checked frock and spotless white apron, and the sensible face beneath the red-checked turban. So she and Guy were not to be entirely alone. That made her feel just a little bit better!

The taxi-driver carried their bags into the spacious air-conditioned hall, then as he departed, with a generous tip, Marilyn turned to address Olinda and Guy. 'Would you like a cold drink and a snack while I unpack for you?' she enquired.

Olinda started to nod. The temperature outside had been well into the eighties and a cold drink was precisely what she felt like at that moment. But before she could say so, Guy had closed the gap between them and slipped a firm, warm arm around her waist. Then, to her horror, she heard him say,

'I don't think so, not for the moment, Marilyn. Miss Steven and I would prefer to be alone. Perhaps if you could just show us to the master bedroom. . .'

With a discreet, knowing smile, Marilyn turned slightly and pointed one finger down the marble-tiled corridor. 'It's down there on the left, sir, and it's all prepared. I think you should find it comfortable.'

'Excellent,' purred Guy in response, pausing to bestow a suggestive silken smile upon Olinda's suddenly flushed face. 'Miss Steven and I will have a snack of something later. Perhaps in a couple of hours or so.'

Then a moment later, Olinda was being steered—in spite of her rigid attempts to resist—down the corridor to the waiting bedroom.

CHAPTER FIVE

'WHAT the devil do you think you're up to?'

As soon as they were inside the bedroom, Olinda wrenched herself free from his embrace, the sheer, desperate force of the manoeuvre sending her catapulting across the tiled floor. She staggered against the wall and swung round to confront him. 'Don't you think you're assuming just a little too much?'

'Not at all, *chérie*.' He was unperturbed. 'It is natural, in the circumstances, for us to want to be alone. Have you forgotten already that we are lovers?'

'No, we are not! We are merely pretending! And, in my opinion, you're taking things a little too far!'

Guy shook his head slowly and regarded her flushed face. 'What's the matter, have you no passion in your soul? Have you no imagination? You have evidently never had a passionate affair, or there would be no need for me to explain the driving urgency that two lovers feel to be alone.'

At least about one thing he was right. Olinda had never had a passionate affair in her life—nor any other kind of affair, come to that. As to his queries about imagination and passion, she had enough of the former to feel thoroughly threatened, and it was the passion in *his* soul that was currently troubling her.

And Guy, it seemed, could read her like a book. With a rakish smile, he turned the key in the door, then removed it from the lock and dropped it in his pocket. 'Since you are such an innocent, I see I shall have to instruct you.' To Olinda's consternation, he shrugged off his jacket and dropped it casually on to the back of a chair. Then, loosening his tie, he sat down on the bed and, one by one, pulled off his shoes. 'We must deal immediately, *ma chère*, with this lamentable gap in your education.'

The man was outrageous! What was he suggesting? Olinda felt herself freeze against the wall, as inscrutable blue eyes slid round to challenge her. All at once, her brain and her eyes were filled with the overpowering image of the huge white bed and the dark, virile man who so effortlessly dominated it. She scrabbled for control. 'What are you talking about? And kindly explain why you've just locked the door!'

'Privacy, *ma chère*. We do not wish to be disturbed.' He unbuttoned the collar and cuffs of his shirt and leaned back casually against the pile of soft pillows. His hair was glossy and as black as midnight against the snow-white lace-trimmed linen, and his forearms, as he pushed back the sleeves of his shirt, were muscular and deeply bronzed. He patted the coverlet beside him. 'Come *chérie*. Come and sit here.'

'What for?' Olinda hadn't moved a centimetre. She was still standing defensively with her back against the wall, the alarm in her laced with a burgeoning anger that he should dare to threaten her this way.

'Why, in order that I may instruct you in the mysteries of sexual love. You are, if I have understood correctly, blissfully ignorant of the mechanics of such things.'

'And I have every intention of remaining so!' Olinda glared at him ferociously. If he should as much as make one move towards her, she would scream the damned house down!

But he did not move. Instead he smiled. 'Calm down, Olinda. There is nothing to fear.' Then, deliberately, studiedly holding her gaze, he undid another two buttons of his shirt, exposing a deep triangle of sunburnished chest. 'The manner of instruction I have in mind, I assure you, is purely theoretical, not practical. What are you thinking?' he demanded amusedly, observing the relieved and faintly foolish look that filtered warmly across her face. 'That I was intending perhaps to forcibly ravish you? You must consider me desperate indeed,' he added mockingly, 'that I should resort to such savage measures.'

'And what else is a respectable girl supposed to think?' Olinda shot back at him, her eyes like flints. Inexplicably, she felt insulted. The word 'desperate' had an unchivalrous ring. 'When a man locks her in a bedroom and pockets the key, I think she can be excused for making that assumption!'

'So that was what worried you? But you must not leap to conclusions. The locking of the door, *ma petite*, was for the benefit of Marilyn. To underline our need to be alone, without any fear of interruption.' He raised one eyebrow and assured her calmly, 'It was not intended to alarm you.'

Olinda looked into his eyes and half believed him. That he had never intended to force himself on her, undoubtedly, was true. Guy de Chevalley, the great seducer, would have no taste for, nor indeed any need

of primitive displays of brutish strength. His conquests
would rely on the subtleties of charm and on that potent
sexual allure that he radiated from every pore.

As to his claim that he had not intended to alarm
her, she would take that with a pinch of salt. When it
came to the arena of psychological games-playing, Guy,
she was fast learning, was a skilled and adept player.
Ruthless too. Cunning and unprincipled. He would
hesitate at absolutely nothing to ensure that he kept the
upper hand.

Remember that, she counselled herself firmly, as she
gathered herself together and crossed to sit beside him.
She had chosen to take on a truly lethal adversary. She
would underestimate him at her peril.

She forced a cool smile and enquired matter-of-
factly, 'So what was this instruction you were intending
to give me? Go ahead and tell me. I'm all ears.'

He leaned back against the pillows and clasped his
hands behind his head, so that the thin white shirt
stretched tautly across his chest. 'It seems to me you
desperately need instructing in the basics of how to
conduct an affair. Or rather, how to *pretend* to conduct
one,' he corrected himself. 'Since the whole point of
this exercise is to draw attention to ourselves, we must
make sure that our little act is convincing.' He paused
to bestow a derogatory smile. 'Your performance on
the journey here, I have to say, was quite lamentable.'

'In what way?' Hot colour rose to Olinda's cheeks as
she caught the wicked glint in his eye. Hadn't she
permitted him to hold her hand, even peck her on the
cheek a couple of times? 'I thought my performance
was perfectly adequate!'

'That's what I feared.' Guy frowned. 'And that's why we need to have this conversation. We are supposed to be lovers, *ma chère* Olinda, two people who know each other's most intimate secrets, who have lain naked together, who have performed the act of love. We are two hungry people who crave one another, whose bodies ignite at a single glance—not two casual, awkward acquaintances who wince and draw away from one another whenever they accidentally touch!'

His graphic exposition had made her face flame, and a warm light glow in the pit of her stomach at the pictures and sensations it had somehow conjured up. 'Surely it's enough,' she protested weakly, 'that we're here and living together in this house. I really don't see any need for anything more than that.'

'Then I'm afraid, *chérie*, I must disabuse you. Your innocence is charming, but your ignorance must be corrected. If this scheme is to have any chance of working, then we must make the effort to perform our parts properly.' He paused to fix her with a warning look. 'And, if you remember, you pledged your full co-operation.'

Olinda nodded and smiled a secret smile. That was not all she had pledged, if he only knew it! Demurely she told him, 'Yes, I remember, and I'll co-operate.'

'That would be most wise.' He relaxed back against the pillows. 'You can always comfort yourself with the fact that our performance is for public consumption only. When the two of us are on our own it's entirely our own choice how we behave.'

'In that case, if you don't mind, I'll take this opportunity to settle into my own room now.' Olinda slid from the bed and held out her hand. 'Give me the key,' she ordered sharply. 'Your instructive little lesson has just been concluded.'

Guy smiled and slowly shook his head. 'My lesson may be over, but you're staying right here. This, *chérie*, is your room—and mine.'

'But you just said——! Surely you don't expect that I should actually share a bedroom with you?'

'Not only do I expect it, I'm afraid I must insist upon it. What on earth would Marilyn think if we were to sleep in separate rooms. No, no, *ma chérie*, we cannot take the risk. Such information could get around.'

He was right, of course, Olinda confessed with sinking heart, cursing herself for her own naïveté. It had never occurred to her to consider such details when she had thrown herself so recklessly into this folly!

She folded her arms across her chest, belligerent and defensive at the same time. 'Well, I'm sure as hell not going to share a bed with you, so don't think you can talk me into that one! There's no way you're going to convince me that that's an essential part of the plan!'

'I wouldn't try to, *chère* Olinda. And, in fact, I have already worked out a solution to that particular problem.' Guy leaned back more comfortably against the pillows and fixed her with an infuriating smile. 'The mattress on this bed is two singles linked together—so all we have to do is unlink them and lay one of them on the floor, then reassemble them in the morning. That will involve dismantling the bedclothes, of course. . .' he paused before adding with devilish amusement '. . .but I doubt very much that Marilyn would expect to find the bedclothes each morning in pristine condition.'

Olinda's lips pursed with disapproval. He had such a lascivious turn of phrase and such a blatant disregard for the niceties of decorum. The way he had made such a point of referring to her as 'Miss Steven' when speaking to Marilyn earlier, for example—not even a glimmer of pretence at some legitimate liaison. And, though she could appreciate that that was all part of the plan—it was essential that their identities should not be hidden—it had rankled with her all the same.

Whoever would believe of her now that she was a girl of the highest moral character?

'Don't worry, *mignonne*.' Guy seemed to read her mind. 'If all goes well, we should manage to tie all this up before the stories about us have time to spread. It is most unlikely,' he added with dry humour, 'that your friends and family in England will ever learn about our little affair.'

Olinda flashed him a look of disfavour, though she was secretly praying that he was right. That her mother might learn about this sordid involvement was a fear that, more than once, had entered her head. After what Guy de Chevalley had done to Dolores, her mother would probably never forgive her, no matter what damage she brought down on his head.

'As far as the local populace are concerned,' Guy continued in the same cavalier vein, 'I can assure you, no one will turn a hair. Holiday romances are meat and drink to them. As for Marilyn,' he enlarged, homing in with uncanny accuracy on the very issue that had sparked all this off, 'she's not going to bother her head.

I can tell just by looking at her that she's a woman of the world.'

And he was such an expert on women, of course! To her chagrin, Olinda suspected he was probably right. Yet the recollection of the little scene he had enacted in response to the woman's offers of refreshment still made her burn with embarrassment inside. Miss Steven and I would prefer to be alone. Perhaps you could just show us to the master bedroom. . . Then the silken smile as he had gone on to elaborate that they would be occupied for the next couple of hours!

She turned on him now in hot resentment. 'Woman of the world or not, there was no need for you to go to such painstaking lengths to give her the totally spurious impression that we were about to embark on some sort of sexual marathon!'

The wide mouth dimpled at the corners. 'I would scarcely call a couple of hours a marathon.' Guy sat up and shook his dark head slowly. 'You indeed have much to learn about love.'

No doubt she had, but he would never be her tutor! Nothing in the world was surer than that!

She took a step back as he slid from the bed and stood for a moment smiling down at her. 'So what do you suggest we do to pass what remains of this couple of hours of ours?' He glanced at the gold Rolex Oyster at his wrist. 'An hour and a half can hang rather heavy—unless, of course, you've had second thoughts about indulging in this sexual marathan you were talking about?'

Olinda's gaze was studiously on his face, hating the blatant mockery that shone there. How was she ever to accomplish her task of manipulating him to the point of confiding in her? The man was about as manipulable as a twenty-foot shark! And, what was more, she had the uncomfortable sensation that *she* was the one, yet again, being manipulated, as, without ever dropping his eyes from her face, he began to undo the remaining buttons of his shirt. With one movement he removed the shirt from his trousers, so that the front fell wide to expose his broad chest.

It was a quite spectacular chest, she observed, without quite daring to look directly. And, suddenly, this expanse of prime male flesh was doing extraordinary things to her pulse rate.

She swallowed drily and kept looking straight at him. 'And what are you doing now, if I may ask?'

Without answering, he slid the shirt from his shoulders—shoulders quite as handsome as his chest—then turned briefly to drop the discarded garment on to a nearby chair. Then, as he turned back, his hands were on the belt of his trousers, making Olinda's confused heart jump anxiously in her chest.

'What were you hoping I was doing, *chérie*? Since you are so disobliging, I am going to have a shower.'

Then he smiled and, before she realised what was happening, he had stepped towards her and was drawing her into his arms. The blue eyes burned down into hers for a moment and then, all at once, his lips were kissing her.

It was not a particularly passionate kiss; his lips against hers were gentle and soft, and the firm, light pressure of his arms barely seemed to restrain her at all. And yet, the very instant his mouth covered hers, excitement, like a bright light, flooded within her, drowning at birth any thought of resistance, sending her senses up in flames.

Her form seemed to mould itself to his almost naturally, and no sensation had ever felt more erotic than the hard, heated pressure of his body against hers. She could feel the broad chest gently crushing her breasts through the thin cotton fabric of her dress, the tantalising thrust of the masculine hips and, above all, the unforced, spine-tingling strength of the encompassing arms that held her to close.

Her eyes had fluttered closed like petals and her lips were suddenly slack with longing. It was as though some demon had entered into her and taken her over, body and soul. For one moment all hatred in her vanished and a single, overpowering emotion enthralled her. She wanted him—to possess him and for him to possess her—as she had never wanted any man before.

But, even as she shrank in realisation of this madness, the arms about her were loosening their grip, and the lips that had so impaired her sanity were softly detaching themselves from hers. Then long-lashed blue eyes burned down into hers as a slow smile spread across his face.

'That was just my way of putting the seal on our partnership. So much more agreeable than a mere handshake, don't you think?'

Then he was turning and striding off towards the bathroom, Olinda watching his progress with still wildly beating heart. She had just been taught a powerful lesson. This man was even more lethal than she had thought!

* * *

At least, as regarded their sleeping arrangements, Guy proved uncharacteristically chivalrous.

Somewhat to Olinda's surprise, on that first night together he had insisted that he take the mattress on the floor, leaving Olinda with the luxurious bed to herself. He had then proceeded to fall, more or less instantly, into a deep and untroubled sleep, whereas she had tossed fitfully for ages before sleep had finally come to claim her.

In spite of her resolution, made that morning in the ladies' room, to conquer her scruples over what she was doing, she still could not quite quell the uneasiness within her. Dealing with gossip columnists wasn't something she had any taste for. In truth she despised rags like the *Bugle*. And it gave her an uncomfortably creepy-crawly feeling to think that she had actually thrown in her lot with them.

What was more, the practical side of the whole business was a worry. Olinda was a scientist who felt at home when she was working within the clear-cut parameters of her discipline. She simply wasn't used to all this intrigue. She found the tangled mechanics of it rather daunting.

For example, she had agreed with Aurora Benjamin, the gossip columnist from the *Bugle*, that any information she managed to prise from Guy she would mail immediately back to Miami, and that as soon as she arrived in Barbados she would let the columnist know where she was staying in case the *Bugle* had cause to get in touch with her.

Now, in the thought-provoking wee small hours of darkness, Olinda's mind was plagued by a thousand worries. She had agreed to let the columnist know where she was staying on the assumption that she and Guy would be checking into a hotel. That assumption, of course, had proved mistaken, and there was no way she dared allow anyone from the *Bugle* to contact her at the villa.

She tossed and turned. She must write to this woman immediately and warn her that some other arrangement must be made. But how would she be able to get word to her with Guy breathing down her neck all the time? Come to that, did she have it in her to play the spy without making him suspicious? And, of equally pressing and crucial importance, what was her best strategy for winning his confidence?

All these questions were still unanswered, as exhaustion finally overtook her and she drifted gratefully into sleep, her last thought being, as unconsciousness claimed her, that her previously quiet and trouble-free existence was rapidly being replaced by a nightmare.

By contrast with Olinda's troubled state of mind, Guy appeared not have a worry in his head, as next morning over breakfast on the veranda he launched with gusto into their charade.

Olinda was obliged to put on as brave a face as possible as he subjected her to an onslaught of kisses and caresses—which, if highly irksome to their recipient, at least provided Marilyn with a little light entertainment. And even Olinda had to grant that he played his part convincingly. No doubt he had performed the role of lover so often that he could virtually play it in his sleep.

For her part she carefully played along with him, initiating nothing, but not rebuffing him either. Little by little she must appear to be won over. Little by little she must persuade him to trust her.

They spent the morning on the beach.

Silver Cove, their villa, she discovered, was just a stone's throw away from the blue Caribbean, and there was a tiny stretch of palm-fringed beach set aside for their exclusive use. As Olinda stretched out on one of the sunbeds, resplendent in her pink bikini, and gazed up at the blazing, cloudless sky, she allowed herself a flush of well-being at finding herself in such a place. In spite of Guy and all the associated complications, this island was like stumbling into paradise. And now, for a blissful couple of hours, she would simply close her eyes to his presence and pretend she had it all to herself!

But a couple of minutes were all she got.

All at once a shadow had fallen over her and a deep dark velvety voice was enquiring, 'Shall I oil you, *chérie*? It would be advisable. The sun is stronger than you realise.'

With a flash of irritation, momentarily forgetting herself, Olinda sat up with a jerk and glared at him. 'I don't need you to oil me!' she snapped. 'I'm perfectly able to do it myself!'

On the short stroll down from the villa to the beach he had worn a T-shirt and faded black shorts. She had walked behind him, looking anywhere but at him, acutely conscious of his semi-nakedness—not to mention her own, beneath her loose beach top. He had now shed the T-shirt and the shorts, and stood over her in a pair of scanty blue swimming trunks that vaunted as much as they concealed his generously proportioned masculine charms.

And indeed he was exceptionally well made. Broad shoulders, strong arms, a magnificent chest and a pair of iron-hard, sinewy legs, liberally garnished with silky black hairs. With a concentrated effort Olinda tore her eyes away from the deeply tanned, muscular, bulging thighs, more or less on a level with her eyes, and tried to concentrate on what he was saying.

'Come, come *ma chère*, that is no way to respond to the overtures of your lover.' His tone was momentarily sharp, as he lowered his tall frame on to the sunbed beside her and picked up her bottle of tanning lotion from where she had dropped it in the sand. 'You may think we're private here, but who knows what secret eyes may be watching us?' He cast an elaborate glance towards the fringe of palm trees that ran along the inside perimeter of the beach, then extended the gesture out to sea, where a colourful posse of small boats bobbed. 'Surely you do not expect those whose job it is to spy on us to announce their presence with rocket flares and flags?'

'Of course not,' she agreed. 'I was being silly.' Then her stomach clenched strangely as Guy laid down the bottle and indicated to her to roll over on to her stomach.

'Except when we are in our room at the villa,' he was saying, as obediently, stiffly, she did as he bade, 'we can never be certain of being alone. Therefore we must at all times keep up the appearance of being lovers, or else it is pointless us being here at all.'

As he finished the sentence, his hand came down on her, making her flesh jump and the breath catch in her throat. It was the coolness of the lotion, she told herself firmly. Nothing whatsoever to do with his touch.

Yet he had a remarkably delicate and pleasurable touch. His long, strong fingers against her bare back moved with a supple, sensuous fluidity, firm yet light, thorough yet tantalising, making her relax almost abandonedly against the canvas of the sunbed. With one hand he swept up her shoulder-length brown hair, making the hairs on the back of her neck stand up and sending a shiver of strangely shocking sensation skittering across her scalp.

Next he turned his attention to her arms, working his magic from shoulder to wrist, and she was just about to breathe a sigh of relief that he had finished his dastardly ministrations when she felt him pour some lotion over the backs of her thighs.

It was at that point that she had to focus her thoughts elsewhere—anywhere but on what he was doing. As his fingers swept expertly over the sensitive flesh, from bikini boundary to ankle, causing ripples of wicked sensation to dart through her, it took every shred of self-control she possessed to remain still and passive beneath the onslaught.

For he was doing it deliberately, she was sure of it. Teasing her, playing with her, delighting in the fact that for the moment she was helpless in his thrall.

Fixedly, she stared down at the sand and willed herself to endure until he had finished. Don't worry, de Chevalley, she vowed grimly to herself. I shall pay you back for this as well!

Then, at last, he was rising from the sunbed and tossing the bottle of lotion down beside her. 'No need for you to return the favour,' he was saying with that familiarly sardonic amused twist in his voice. 'I know you're simply dying to get your hands on me, but personally I never bother with sun creams and things.' He threw himself down casually on the sand beside her. 'However, just say the word whenever you're ready and I'll be only too glad to oil your other side as well.'

'How kind.' Her tone did not disguise her true feelings. Then she waited a moment and suggested neutrally, 'Unless you have any other plans, I'd like to go into Bridgetown after lunch.'

'That's OK with me. Any special reason? Anything you particularly want to do there?'

Olinda shook her head. 'No, nothing special,' she lied. 'Just have a look at the shops and maybe buy some postcards.' And make a brief stop at the post office, she added silently, to mail a letter to Miami.

'OK. Bridgetown it is.' Guy rolled over on his side to fix her with a warning look. 'I hope you're not working on some dastardly plot to try and lose me in the crowd?' He smiled thinly. 'That would be a waste of time.'

'Would I do a thing like that?' Olinda mimicked innocence, as with what she hoped was a cool look she returned his smile.

But inwardly her heart was beating nervously and she was feeling anything but cool. For it was nothing as innocent as a game of hide and seek she was planning. Somehow she had to conquer her nerves and her scruples and make her first urgent contact with Aurora at the *Bugle*.

* * *

After lunch, while Guy was changing, Olinda locked herself in the bathroom and hurriedly scribbled a note to Aurora Benjamin on a couple of the complimentary sheets of notepaper she had thoughtfully removed from her hotel room in Miami. In essence it was an urgent plea to the columnist on no account to try to contact her at the villa, but to write to her care of the *poste restante* in Bridgetown should she have some pressing need to get in touch with her.

She read and re-read what she had written, nervously checking that the message was clear. If through some blunder of the *Bugle*'s Guy were to discover what she was up to, her life wouldn't be worth a bag of chopped liver.

With a sigh she stuffed the letter into an envelope and paused to glance at her reflection in the mirror. All this cloak and dagger stuff made her feel decidedly edgy. It just didn't suit her. It went against her nature. And yet, she reminded herself, frowning into the mirror, it was she who had initiated this whole venture. And, currently, in the cloak and dagger stakes, she was the one who was making the running.

Among other things, she had deliberately failed to reveal her relationship with Dolores to Aurora, fearing that if the columnist were aware of this detail her story might be forced to take on a new angle. For, as a journalist, Aurora would be unable to ignore the added interest that would be generated by the revelation that Guy's traducer was not just some anonymous, spiteful girlfriend, but the sister of his dead fiancée. Such a twist could lead to all sorts of sordid complications, and the situation was already quite sordid enough.

And it was this seedy, sordid aspect of the whole business that continued, above all, to bother Olinda. It was all very well her telling herself that she was simply playing the game according to Guy's cynical rules. These rules were not the rules by which she prided herself on living. They were the rules of the gutter and, as such, they tainted her.

For a moment she hesitated. Should she add a postscript to her letter, saying that she had changed her mind? Should she back out now while she still had time?

In the mirror her frown deepened. It was too late for that. She had already told them all about Dolores. Like it or not, she was in up to her neck. She might as well face up to that.

With a sigh she licked the envelope and sealed it shut. Think positively! she commanded herself, stuffing the sealed envelope into her bag. She scowled at her reflection and swung the bag over her shoulder. Think of Dolores and what Guy did to her. Surely that's all the justification you need.

Guy was waiting for her out on the terrace, looking cool and quite infuriatingly handsome in slim white trousers and an open-necked white shirt. The blue eyes looked her up and down, as he rose from the cane chair where he'd been sitting, seeming subtly to cast admiring approval on the lemon and white striped dress she'd changed into.

Then he was gallantly offering her his arm and leading her down the wooden staircase to where a white hire Cadillac was waiting. 'Mission Bridgetown,' he pronounced with a smile, causing Olinda's eyes to dart away guiltily and her fingers to tauten around the strap of her bag. Then he was pulling open the passenger door for her and she was climbing quickly inside. At least, his mood seemed equable, she consoled herself. Perhaps, in spite of all her worries, it might not prove too difficult to do what she must do.

His good mood continued throughout the afternoon, as he took her on a light-hearted tour of the capital. 'They say Bridgetown is the most English of all Caribbean cities,' he told her, as they paused at a little outdoor café for some pumpkin fritters and a long cool drink. 'You should be feeling quite at home here.'

Olinda glanced round the dusty square, with its colourful shop-fronts and sun-scorched cobblestones, and threw him an amused look in response. 'Oh, yes, it's just like England,' she joked. 'In every detail, right down to the weather!'

'You can't expect everything. The English climate is unique,' Guy responded, laughing along with her. 'But I'll bet you never expected, right here in the Caribbean, to find yourself standing in the middle of Trafalgar Square——'

'—gazing up at a mini-version of Nelson's Column,' Olinda finished for him, shaking her head as she remembered the surprise he had sprung on her just half an hour ago. 'That was really quite a revelation. For a moment I thought I was back in London!' She glanced curiously across at him. 'How come you know this place so well?'

He shrugged, as though there were nothing more normal than that one should be well acquainted with such exotic locations. 'I've visited the island before,' he told her. 'It's one of my most favourite places in the world.'

'I reckon it could grow to be one of mine as well.' She glanced round her, her tone wistful as she said it. The more she saw of the island the more she loved it, but, unlike him, she was never likely to be back again.

He read her mind. 'Who knows?' he said. 'Stranger things have been known to happen.'

For a moment, as their eyes met, a flash of sympathy passed between them and, without thinking, Olinda responded to his smile.

'In the meantime, I intend to make very sure that you make the most of this particular visit.' He held her eyes a moment longer. 'Just because of our "arrangement", there's no reason why we shouldn't enjoy ourselves.'

Olinda glanced away and took a mouthful of her pineapple juice, reluctant to go along with this unlikely proposition. Since the moment he had first announced that he would be accompanying her to Barbados, she had renounced all hope of having a good time and resigned herself to two weeks of misery. But, in fact, this afternoon she had enjoyed herself thoroughly. When he was not being dictatorial, Guy was an enchanting companion.

She checked this thought instantly, surprised by her own naïveté. Of course, when he wanted to be, he could be enchanting. That was why he was such an accomplished seducer!

He was glancing at his watch. 'I suggest we make our next stop the post office. You said you wanted to send off these postcards you've just written and I'm not sure what time it closes.'

To her annoyance Olinda flushed at this reminder of her deception and of how easily he had accepted her story. She drained her glass to hide her confusion and nodded, 'OK. That's fine by me.'

Fifteen minutes or so later they left the little café and headed on foot in the direction of the post office. All at once, Olinda's heart was beating faster and little shivers of apprehension were trickling down her spine. Somehow she had to get the letter to Aurora posted, but how on earth would she managed to do it if Guy insisted on coming into the post office with her?

For once, however, the gods were with her. Even as she scrabbled for some excuse that would keep him out of her hair for five minutes, Guy cut through her thoughts and calmly suggested, 'If you think you can manage on your own, I'll just nip over to that liquor store across the street and get us a bottle of rum for tonight.'

Relief rushed through her. 'Good idea. I'll wait for you outside when I'm finished.'

Hardly able to believe her good luck, she dived into the fan-cooled interior of the post office and joined what looked like the shortest queue. God—or perhaps the devil—willing, she would have finished her task before he had finished his!

The queue seemed to inch forward almost painfully slowly, but at last it was her turn at the counter. Then, armed with her stamps, she retired to a quiet corner, removed the sealed envelope from her bag and swiftly stuck on the required postage. With shaking hand she returned the envelope to her bag, then dealt quickly and efficiently with the postcards she had bought to provide herself with an acceptable cover. Then, her heart still pounding, she looked around, searching anxiously for the mail box.

As her eye fell upon it, she hurried forward, one hand hovering over her bag. Then she was grabbing the letter and shoving it into the mailbox, to be followed, less nervously, by the postcards.

There was sweat on her brow as she turned away and a sense of weak relief in her heart. But in the very next instant her blood seemed to freeze as her eyes fell on the tall, dark figure in white, who was standing watching her from the doorway. Oh, lord, she thought in sudden panic. Had he seen her post the letter?

She walked on unsteady legs towards him, hardly daring to look him in the face, hardly even daring to breathe. But all he said as she came alongside him was, 'Did you get everything done? Come on, let's go, then.'

As he offered her his arm, without thinking, she took it and followed him out into the vivid sunshine that reflected the renewed warm relief in her heart. But in truth her relief was not exclusively due to the fact that she had posted her letter with impunity. That no damage had been done to this new rapport between them was equally a cause for quiet celebration.

Simply because it makes it easier for me to gain his confidence, she told herself firmly.

But as they headed arm in arm down the dusty street, already one secret corner of her heart knew that was no longer entirely true.

CHAPTER SIX

OLINDA took a mouthful of her delicious planter's punch and glanced at Guy across the candlelit table. 'So how many spies have you spotted so far?' she enquired, smiling.

He was dressed in a pair of black linen trousers, a white linen jacket, white shirt and bow tie, and in the softly flickering light of the candles the sometimes harsh lines of his face were subtly softened and enhanced. As he smiled, his teeth seemed very white and the blueness of his eyes was intense and startling. 'None yet,' he conceded. 'They're keeping a low profile. But don't worry, the night is still young.'

That much was true. It was barely half an hour since they had arrived for an evening at the Humming Bird Club, one of the island's more exclusive nightspots. Naturally, they were seated at one of the better tables arranged around the perimeter of the tiny dance floor— a twenty-dollar bill, exchanged with barely a rustle, had immediately secured them this special privilege—and Olinda, unaccustomed to such glamorous places, with their seductive semi-darkness and soft, throbbing music, was literally loving every minute of it.

The intention behind their coming here had not, however, been purely pleasure. It had been Guy's idea, and the intention was to try and lure his enemies out into the open. In the past few days since their arrival on the island he had been convinced on a couple of separate occasions—once on the beach and once back at the villa—that somebody was watching them. Here at the nightclub he was hoping to unmask them.

'In a small confined area like the Humming Bird,' he had reasoned, 'they won't find it quite so easy to keep hidden. It's going to be that much easier for us to spot anyone who's behaving in a suspicious fashion.'

Olinda shook her head and laid down her glass. 'It beats me how you expect to tell the difference between your own paid spies from the detective agency and the ones who are supposed to be tailing you illicitly.' She threw him a faintly teasing smile. 'But then I suppose that in such matters you're more experienced than I am.'

Guy raised one jet-black devil's wing eyebrow and met her eyes with a lazy, knowing smile. 'I fear I am more experienced than yourself in many matters, *chérie*,' he told her. 'Perhaps that is why I find your innocence so charming.' He allowed his eyes to drift appreciatively over her. 'Although you are looking just a little less innocent this evening.'

Olinda felt a blush creep up from her neck as the blue gaze paused at her naked shoulders, then swept unhurriedly around her neckline, caressing the soft outline of her breasts. For their evening out she had chosen to wear a favourite multi-coloured dress with an off-the-shoulder top and full, swirling skirt, her waist cinched in with a broad matching belt, and a pretty gold pendant, a gift from her mother, glistening at her throat.

In the past, she had always worn the dress more

demurely, the elasticated neckline sitting loosely
around her shoulders, but tonight, on an impulse, she
had been a little bolder, arranging it a couple of inches
lower, more as its designer had intended. Sophisti-
cation, not seduction, had been her main aim, but
clearly Guy was more impressed by the latter effect!

He smiled across at her. 'It suits you, *chérie*. This
evening you are even more desirable than usual.'

She met his eyes, feeling a faint shiver go through
her. 'You'll spoil me with all these compliments,' she
joked. 'Remember, we down-to-earth English girls
aren't used to all this Gallic charm.'

Over the past few days their rapport had deepened
and she found no problem in being free and easy with
him—except when he looked at her like that. For the
power of that blue gaze could turn her limbs to putty
and make the blood burn like white fire in her veins.

It's just a physical thing, she kept telling herself
bravely, a chemical reaction you can do nothing about.
He is, unfortunately, just one of those men who has
this uncanny power to affect women that way.

Of course, in other circumstances, she reassured
herself stoutly, she would simply and instantly have
rebuffed him. For if she cared to she could easily
override her responses. The only thing that was stopping her was that she needed to charm him. It was all a
carefully calculated part of her plan.

And her plan, so far, was working perfectly. Guy had
responded to her change in attitude towards him with
the uninhibited enthusiasm of a compulsive seducer,
exchanging her smiles for kisses and her glances for

caresses, yet never once attempting to step over the boundary which Olinda had firmly set in her mind.

This latter detail had somewhat surprised her, for she had feared she might have to fight him off. But with Guy, she was fast learning, one ought never to make assumptions. He was about as predictable as a basket of kittens.

He continued to watch her, the blue eyes teasing. 'So are you glad I insisted on coming along with you? You must admit you're having a better time with me than you'd have had with that other boyfriend of yours, Elliot.'

Olinda blinked a little at his arrogance, but she could not deny that there was truth in what he said. Over the past few days he had stood by his promise to make sure that she enjoyed herself. He seemed to have a natural talent for having a good time, and for ensuring that those around him did too. There had never been a single dull moment.

Olinda was loath to acknowledge this, however, so instead she picked him up on one small detail. 'Elliot was not my boyfriend.' Her tone was clipped. 'He was simply a friend, as I've told you before.'

'I'm glad to hear it.' He continued to watch her. 'And do you have other Elliots back home?'

'If you mean men friends, yes, I have a few.'

'But no one special?'

'Not at the moment.'

'Not at the moment—then there has been once?'

It really was none of his damned business and she was almost on the point of telling him so. But for some reason, instead, she found herself answering, 'Once there was. At least, I thought he was special. It turned out I was wrong.'

She felt him smile. 'That's what I thought. That explains why you're so wary.' He paused for a moment, surveying her closely, so that she flushed and could not meet his eyes. 'You must learn to be more trusting. A girl like you really ought to have someone special in her life.' Then he dumbfounded her totally as he added, 'But you realise, of course, you're never going to find him if you keep wasting your time on men like Elliot?'

And what was that supposed to mean? She blinked accusingly across at him. 'What's wrong with men like Elliot?' she demanded.

'Nothing in the least. For someone else. But not, *ma chère* Olinda, for you. What you need is a different type of man altogether.'

As he leaned unexpectedly across the table and took a firm hold of her hand, Olinda made an effort to snatch it away. 'And how would *you* know what I need? You don't even know the first thing about me!'

But, as he rose to his feet, he was drawing her up too, eyes like smouldering blue fires flickering into hers. 'Let me illustrate something of what I mean. Come, *chérie*, let us dance.'

Her nerves were suddenly jangling as he led her on to the dance floor, and she could scarcely control the beating of her heart as Guy drew her softly into his arms. At the firm, sure touch of his hand at her waist something within her seemed to judder and the scent of his clean-shaven jaw against her cheek was raising tiny goosebumps all over her.

Was this what he had meant? The demonstration he

had intended? Was he out to show her that he was capable of affecting her as no man had ever affected her before?

As her heart thudded within her, he was speaking softly, his breath a whisper against her hair. 'You see, your claim that I know nothing about you is really a little wide of the mark. I know a great deal more about you, *chérie*, than you appear to think.'

Olinda blinked her eyes upwards to look into his face, feeling a sudden cold flash of alarm within her. Had he uncovered her secrets? Did he know who she was? Or, worse, had he found out what she was up to?

But the cobalt blue eyes were smiling down at her as he went on to elaborate, 'How could it be otherwise? For the past few days we have been living in each other's pockets. At such close proximity one learns a lot about a person.' As she glanced away, he caught her chin with his finger and forced her to meet his eyes again. 'I think you have grown to know me a little too. You no longer believe I am such a monster.'

Olinda shrugged uneasily. Alas, it was true. With each day that passed she was finding it more difficult to continue to view him, as she had done previously, as one step removed from the devil incarnate. On the contrary, to her consternation, she kept finding things to like in him—which perhaps was why, in spite of the growing uneasiness between them, she had made no attempt to prise any dark secrets out of him.

She had tried telling herself that the reason for that was simply that the opportunity had not arisen, but increasingly that argument was growing thin. This lack of purpose on her part was starting to worry her. It also made her feel deeply guilty.

As he continued to hold her chin with his finger, she met his bold blue gaze with her own steady grey one. 'And am I right or wrong if I believe you're not a monster? As I already told you, I've been mistaken before.'

Guy smiled mysteriously and drew her more closely to him, so that she could no longer see his eyes. 'I'll be whatever you want. If you like monsters, I'll be a monster. If you prefer something more cuddly, I'll be your teddy bear.'

Olinda leaned against him, feeling more confused than ever. For she suspected there was truth in that light-hearted statement. Guy de Chevalley was the original chameleon, capable of being whatever he chose.

For the moment, however, she was not allowed to dwell on her confusion. As the music stopped and they made their way back to their table, all at once a female voice was calling out, 'Guy de Chevalley! So it's you, after all! Of all the people to bump into!'

Olinda followed Guy's eyes across the tables to where a blonde-haired woman in a slinky black dress was frantically waving to catch his attention. 'Babette!' he exclaimed, hurrying towards her. And a moment later the two were embracing.

Ten minutes later, after a swift rearrangement of tables, Olinda and Guy and the vivacious Babette, along with Mel, her softly spoken husband, were seated all together, laughing and chatting.

Babette, Olinda had discovered, was an ex-model, a

fact which surprised her not in the slightest. Considering her ravishing prettiness, her tall, slender figure and the immaculate, professional manner of her grooming, it would almost have been surprising had she been anything else. What did come as something of an eye-opener, however, was the revelation that she was a one-time girlfriend of Guy's.

It was not the fact that they had once been lovers that Olinda in any way found hard to take in. Guy's predilection for stunning women was a very well-known and well-documented fact. What surprised her a little and further added to her confusion was the evidence that they were now, quite obviously, good friends. It somehow failed to fit with his public reputation as a man who loved then left the women in his life with almost calculated callousness that an ex-girlfriend should feel so warmly towards him.

And not only an ex-girlfriend, but also her husband, for it was obvious that all three of them were extremely close friends. Perhaps Babette had simply been a lucky exception, Olinda decided, her confusion growing. But a moment later her confusion was doubled.

They were talking about their tastes in music, Babette waxing enthusiastically lyrical about the steel band music of the Caribbean. When Guy agreed, she gave a mischievous giggle. 'I see you're branching out in your musical tastes. I thought you never listened to anything but classical!'

'Not so!' Guy responded to her gibe with humour. 'I happen to have extremely catholic tastes.'

'I've heard you're a bit of an opera buff?' Olinda

interceded without thinking—and was totally unprepared for Babette's reaction.

'Whoever told you that? Guy hates opera! I've tried to convert him on more than one occasion, but he absolutely refuses even to listen to it!'

'But I thought——' Prudently, Olinda stopped short, remembering the source of her false information. It had been Dolores, a firm *aficionada* of Verdi, who had once recounted to her in glorious detail a trip to the Paris Opera House with Guy to see a special performance of *Aida*.

As she sat back in her chair, blinking confusedly, Guy assured her, 'Babette's absolutely right. I'm sure it's a terrible gap in my musical eduction, but I've never been to an opera in my life.'

Olinda shrugged and laughed, 'I must have dreamt it!' But, as the conversation moved on to other topics, her brain was suddenly filled with an irritating question. Why on earth had Dolores invented such a story? It appeared to make no sense at all. And that question inevitably led to another, even more worrying in its implications.

If Dolores had invented the story about the opera, was it possible that she had invented other things as well?

She felt a traitorous clench of excitement at the thought. If Dolores' accusations against Guy were untrue, that would legitimise her own changing feelings for him. She need no longer feel quite so bowed down with guilt.

But then, instantly, she felt ashamed of herself. Dolores was her sister and her first loyalty must be towards her. For the fact that her sister had told one small lie hardly demolished her entire story. For the moment, she told herself sternly, until you have real proof, you'll just have to learn to live with your guilt.

Somehow the conversation had got round to skiing. As Olinda forced her attention back to the present, Babette was asking Guy, as the waiter brought more drinks, 'Do you still have your chalet in the Haute Savoie?' Then, as Guy nodded, she turned to smile at Olinda. 'You really must persuade him to take you there some time, especially if you're keen on skiing.' She slipped her arm affectionaely through her husband's. 'Mel and I had the most fantastic skiing holiday there just a couple of years ago.'

Olinda studiously avoided looking at Guy—she could just imagine his amusement at Babette's suggestion!—and answered, 'As a matter of fact, I'm very fond of skiing, although I'm afraid I'm still very much a beginner.'

'Get Guy to teach you. He's an expert—and a very patient teacher. I'll vouch for that.'

'I'll vouch for that too.' Mel was laughing. 'He was the one who actually got me off the nursery slopes!'

Babette leaned to plant a kiss on his cheek. 'Mel's a wonderful husband, but definitely not an athlete.' She winked at Olinda. 'If he was honest, even now, he prefers the *après*-ski to the actual skiing!'

Mel agreed. 'I like the social side of it—and fortunately, when you're with Guy, there's no shortage of that.'

Olinda smiled in quiet agreement. That was something she already knew. Then she glanced at Babette, as the blonde girl suddenly giggled. 'While we're on the subject of social life, what about that infamous party last year? The one involving a rather well-known lady who wasn't exactly there for the skiing?' She winked across at Olinda and mentioned by name the wife of a prominent French politician. 'A real old-fashioned scandal of a story, that was!' Then she turned again to Guy. 'What exactly happened? You've never told me all the details.'

But as all eyes simultaneously turned to Guy, he seemed reluctant to take up the story. He shook his head. 'It was a messy business. I'm afraid I've forgotten most of the details.'

It was the way he averted his eyes as he spoke, feigning sudden interest in a table near the back, that set off an alarm bell in Olinda's head. As Mel diplomatically took the hint and turned to Babette, inviting her to dance, Olinda's eyes were fastened to Guy's dark profile with a sense of regret mingled with foreboding.

For all at once she had the feeling that he was hiding something, possibly the very story she had set out to look for. And in the very same instant in her heart she knew she had been praying there was no such story to find.

The two couples parted company shortly after midnight after agreeing to meet up again in a couple of days' time and spend a day together deep sea fishing. 'We'll organise the boat from our hotel,' Mel promised, as they climbed into their respective cars. 'I'll give you a call later and we can sort out the details.'

As Guy climbed into the Cadillac beside her, Olinda sank back into the soft, upholstered seat and tried to switch her brain into neutral. The evening had provided her with much to ponder, but right now it was late and she was tired. She would do her pondering tomorrow, she decided, after a good night's sleep.

Guy gunned the engine and glanced across at her. 'Did you enjoy the evening?' he asked.

'Very much,' she said honestly, for between the various revelations she'd had a genuinely good time. 'Babette and Mel are really nice people. I'm glad we bumped into them,' she told him. Then she smiled a wry smile in his direction. 'Too bad, though, you didn't manage to catch any spies!'

Guy pushed the gearstick into drive and winked across at her. 'But that's where you're wrong!' Then, as she blinked in astonishment, he reached for her hand and raised it briefly to his lips. 'I may not have succeeded in actually *catching* any, but I managed to spot them all the same.'

As his lips brushed her fingertips, a shiver went through her, her concentration momentarily shattered. Then it was shattered further as he took her tingling fingers and laid them firmly across his thigh. And she had to struggle to attend to what he was saying as he went on to elaborate, 'There was a red-haired woman and a skinny young guy sitting just a couple of tables away, and definitely with more than just a passing interest in us, I'd say. I managed to have a pretty good look at them and I'm damned sure I'd recognise them if I saw them again.'

'That's good,' she acknowledged, painfully aware that she was barely taking in a word he said. Every atom of her consciousness was focused like a laser on the taut hard strength of the muscular thigh that pressed against the palm of her hand. And she could not move her hand away, for his own hand still held hers prisoner there.

She took a deep breath to still her racing heart, but her voice was husky as she asked him, 'So what's the next step? Where do you go from here?'

He shrugged. 'I'm not exactly sure. I guess I just have to keep a look-out and see if I can spot them again.' He raised her hand once more to his lips, sending another hot shiver lancing through her. Then he squeezed her hand. 'Our plan seems to be working.'

Olinda nodded bemusedly. 'Good,' she answered, not really knowing whether it was good or otherwise, as once more he laid her hand on his thigh.

She was immensely relieved when a short while later the big car turned through the gates of the villa and headed quickly up the driveway. Guy drew up beneath the illuminated veranda, tyres spitting softly, and pulled on the handbrake. Then, just as Olinda was reaching for the door-handle, he he turned to her and slid an arm along the back of her seat.

'Let's not end the evening just yet. How about a quick dip before we turn in?'

As he spoke, his fingers pushed aside her hair to touch the sensitive nape of her neck, and it was as though an electric current shot through her. 'A dip?' she responded a trifle foolishly. 'Do you mean a dip in the sea?'

'A midnight swim.' The blue eyes were twinkling. 'What nicer way to round off the day?' As she hesitated, his fingers caressed the back of her neck, making all the little hairs stand on end. 'Come, Olinda, don't tell me you've never gone for a midnight swim before?'

As a matter of fact she hadn't. She shook her head, not at all certain that she wanted to now. But, before she could answer, he was deciding for her.

'Come on! It's a perfect night for it.'

Then she was being bundled out of the car and he was leading her round to the front of the house and down the pathway that led to the beach.

A sudden thought struck her. 'I haven't got my swimsuit! I'd better go back to the villa and get it.'

But he held her hand firmly and tugged her along behind him. 'It's dark, *chérie*. No one will see us. And besides, it's much better without a swimsuit.'

That was easy enough for him to say! Olinda quailed inwardly as she stumbled behind him, wishing now she'd had the gumption to opt out of this ordeal. Maybe he was used to midnight frolics in the nude, but they were definitely not her style at all!

He grinned at her shamelessly as they stepped on to the sand. 'Come on, I'll race you. Let's see who's in the water first!'

If it had been down to the number of garments each was wearing and the time required to peel them off, Olinda should easily have been first in the water. All she had on was a top and skirt, her sandals and a pair of briefs. Yet Guy somehow managed to divest himself of a suit and shirt, plus a tie, shoes and socks, not to mention a pair of skimpy blue underpants, while she was studiously bent double, still fully clothed, wrestling self-consciously with the strap of her sandal.

As each of his swiftly discarded garments was added

to his pile, Olinda could feel her blushes grow stronger. By the time the blue underpants joined the heap, she was glowing from head to toe.

She heard him say, though she dared not look up at him, 'If you're not in the water in two minutes flat, I'll come back out and drag you in.'

Then, to her tangible relief, he was turning away and sprinting across the sand towards the water. A moment later she raised her eyes discreetly to catch a glimpse of his splendid male body as he hit the water and dived between the waves.

Annoyed with herself, she kicked off her shoes. Don't be such a ninny! she chastised herself. There's no possible danger in going for a swim. Just make sure you keep at a respectable distance from him!

Carefully she slipped off her skirt, then, making a quick check to see if he was watching her—he wasn't!— she pulled her top quickly over her head. She was wearing no bra and she cursed herself now for her unfortunate choice of attire tonight. But at least she was wearing a pair of white cotton briefs, and no way did she intend discarding those! *Semi*-nudity was absolutely as far as she was prepared to go!

She folded her arms across her chest as she headed on firm steps for the water, glad to see Guy was swimming a little way out. With any luck she would have time to immerse herself before he even realised she was on her way.

But as fate would have it, she mistimed her entrance badly. She was up to her waist in the cool clear water when his dark head bobbed up and he waved and called out to her, 'Congratulations! You made it! I was just about to come and get you!'

Cursing him, Olinda abruptly lowered herself up to her shoulders in the water. Then, as he struck out once more towards the horizon in an elegant, seemingly effortless crawl, she felt herself begin to relax a little, and sank back into the clear, cool water.

She had to admit it felt quite delicious, as it swirled and moved softly against her semi-naked body, and there was something extra specially exciting about the balmy, still silence of the night and the fact that nobody was there but them. She swam a few strokes, then rolled over on to her back and gazed up at the huge silver moon. There really was something rather exotic about having the entire Caribbean to oneself!

Almost to oneself, she was swiftly reminded, as a soft splash at her shoulder made her turn round. And suddenly she did not feel quite so relaxed as she found herself looking into a pair of blue eyes.

'How do you like it?' He was smiling down at her, his wet hair tar-black in the moonlight, swept back cleanly from his forehead, throwing his features into dramatic relief. In the pale light his cheekbones seemed almost sculpted, the curve of his nose and the jut of his jaw so firm they might have been hewn from marble. And the droplets of water, like tiny crystals, that were clinging to his thick dark lashes, somehow made the whites of his eyes seem whiter and the cobalt-blue irises deeper and darker.

She gazed into those eyes with a sense of helpless longing, a longing she could barely hold in check. Then, as his arms slid round her waist and he drew her upright, so that she was half standing, half floating in front of him, without even thinking, her arms went round his neck.

If there are any spies watching right now, she thought weakly, they'll have no difficulty in believing that we're lovers for real.

But, in that very same instant, another thought struck her. She frowned at Guy as her heart gave a leap. 'That couple you saw at the club,' she queried. 'When did you spot them? At what point in the evening?'

His brows drew together as he caressed her bare shoulders. 'I can't remember. It was towards the end.'

Olinda swallowed. 'When we were talking about the skiing? Just before Mel and Babette went off to dance?'

Guy shook his head. 'It might have been. Yes, as a matter of fact, I believe it was.' Then as she hugged him, he laughed. 'What's the difference? Why on earth did you want to know?'

'No reason, no reason.' She hugged him tighter. A huge grin had broken out over her face. For suddenly she knew why his attention had wavered when Babette had raised the subject of that Alpine scandal. Not, as Olinda had at first suspected, because he had in any way been feeling guilty, but quite simply because, at that very moment, he had spotted the people who were watching them.

Her heart danced within her. She had been wrong to suspect him. He hadn't been trying to hide anything at all! Then she remembered Dolores' lie about the opera and the significance of Guy's friendship with Babette, his ex-girlfriend. All the bad things she had heard about him simply could not be true! She and the rest of the world had misjudged him!

It was like a great weight slipping from her shoulders. It was not wrong of her to feel for him the way she did. She felt a flood of warmth go rushing through her. He was not, after all, the monster she had feared.

He was smiling down at her. 'I have a confession to make.' And his arms were about her, holding her lightly, as for an instant Olinda felt her heart freeze. Then she breathed again as he went on to tell her, 'I'm afraid I watched you coming down the beach—and I can report that you're a very beautiful woman indeed.'

Olinda blushed, but it was a blush of pleasure, not embarrassment. 'And I watched you too,' she responded, smiling. 'And I can report that you're not a bad-looking man.' Then as their eyes met and held and the cool, caressing fingers moved upwards from her shoulders to tangle with her hair, she could not hold back the gasp of excitement that rose involuntarily to her lips.

'Chérie, chérie.' He was drawing her head backwards, almost violently, to gaze deep into her eyes. And an instant later he was jerking her towards him and she could feel her senses leap and bend within her as his mouth took bold possession of her own.

His mouth on hers was hungry and demanding, yet generous and giving at the same time, igniting in her a raw, sharp hunger that made her moan as she pressed longingly against him.

She had momentarily forgotten that he was naked, and the sudden hard thrust of his arousal against her sent shockwaves of excitement and alarm rushing through her. But if it had been in her mind to pull away from him, that intention was instantaneously overridden as he twined one muscular leg around her, his knee pressing at her waist, holding her firmly against him, while his two hands came round to cover her breasts.

Sharp needles of delight were prickling through her as he moulded and caressed the firm, excited flesh, stirring within her loins an aching longing as his thumbs strummed the swollen, burgeoning peaks.

Her arms wound round him, one hand caressing the firm hard quivering flesh of his shoulders, while the fingers of the other twisted hungrily through his head of thick dark hair. Then as his fingers rhythmically grazed her nipples, the shivering excitement that had been building inside her seemed to be struggling towards a crescendo. Her arms tightened involuntarily as she pressed against him, breathing raggedly between her teeth. Make love to me! Take me! her senses were crying. Please don't torture me like this!

As she moved against him, she could hear him moan softly, and the hands that held her breasts tightened their grip. Then, with a suddenness and a ferocity that made her shudder and sent a shaft of raw, wanton lust jarring through her, his hands were sweeping downwards to her hips, easing the white cotton briefs away.

But then, even as her heart stopped in anticipation, he paused and muttered something incomprehensible in French. Then with strong arms he was scooping up her nerveless body and carrying her towards the shore.

'I think we'd better get dressed, *chérie*,' he murmured, setting her gently on the sand. Then as he bent to kiss her, softly, lingeringly, a sudden wrench of sadness tore at her heart.

For suddenly Olinda realised, as he turned away from her, that this longing within her would never be fulfilled. Though to him she was just one woman among a thousand, a passing diversion, soon to be forgotten, she at that moment would have traded her soul just to hear him murmur one single word of love.

CHAPTER SEVEN

IT WAS madness, of course, Olinda knew that. By allowing herself to feel for Guy as she did she was simply setting herself up for an enormous letdown. For she had never deluded herself for one moment that, for Guy, she was any more than a passing amusement.

It was that old masochistic urge of the Steven women always to fall for the wrong sort of man rising up within her and dragging her down again. Only this time, she thought wryly, she deserved a gold medal. She had known in advance just how dangerous Guy was, but she had believed herself immune to him, protected by her hatred. And yet, without scarcely putting up a fight, she had shed that protection and, like a sacrificial lamb, walked willingly, even eagerly, straight into his arms.

And there was much more at stake here than the mere risk of a heartbreak. More crucially, she feared for her ability to live with herself should this sudden dramatic turnaround of hers prove ill-founded.

That night under a full moon in his arms she had talked herself into believing that Guy was innocent, that Dolores had lied, that the world had misjudged him. In the cold light of day she had been forced to acknowledge that her arguments had been based on instinct and speculation. And her scientifically trained mind demanded something more substantial. What she needed were some hard facts to back up her instincts.

125

Once she had those, she argued to herself ruefully, she could follow her heart to its inevitable ruination.

She laughed bitterly at the irony of the situation, recalling how she had started off looking for evidence to use against him, yet here she was now, one short week later, desperately hoping to uncover something that would finally exonerate him. No wonder she had trouble making sense of her feelings!

And so now in this trial of muddied loyalties Olinda was pledged to find evidence for the defence, a mission that would require every bit as much subtlety as her previous mission on behalf of the prosecution.

Her tactics, however, remained essentially the same. Somehow she would have to prise secrets out of him, only secrets of a very different nature. And then, when she was satisfied, she privately promised herself, she would immediately contact Aurora Benjamin, withdrawing the story she had already told her and severing forever all links with the *Bugle*. Just the thought of that made her sigh with relief.

Initially, not knowing what she was looking for, she made one or two unfortunate false starts. Over dinner that evening, as she plied Guy with questions about his family, hoping some reassuring crumbs of information might accidentally fall her way, he suddenly stopped eating and narrowed his eyes at her.

'You're very curious,' he observed with a slight edge to his voice. 'Perhaps I ought to supply you with a written history of the de Chevalleys.' As she blanched a little, he went on to add, 'I thought industrial espionage was your game? Perhaps you've decided to branch out a little?'

Olinda had cursed herself and tried to shrug it off. 'I'm sorry,' she offered as light-heartedly as she could. 'It's just that you're such an interesting family.' Then, as he raised one dark eyebrow, seeing straight through her flattery, she challenged, 'Besides, you know I'm not an industrial spy. You couldn't still believe anything so ridiculous about me, surely?'

He looked her straight in the eye in that way he had that made her feel he could read what she was thinking. Then, without answering her question, he poured more wine into their glasses. 'Drink, *chérie*. Don't ask so many questions.'

He was not an easy man out of whom to prise confidences, Olinda decided later that night in bed. She would just have to be patient and tread very carefully. Sooner or later he must give something away.

The following morning on the beach she almost made another *faux pas*. There was a fleeting moment when Guy's eyes seemed to darken and she knew she was asking too many questions again. This time, however, she backed off before he could chastise her and adroitly changed the subject without repercussions. But later, as they were having lunch together at the villa, the break she had been angling for finally came.

They had spent most of the morning water-skiing— at least Guy had water-skied, Olinda for the most part had spent the morning dragging herself out of the water.

'Don't worry,' Guy told her, heaping lobster on to her plate. 'You did very well indeed for a first-timer. I feel confident that by tomorrow you'll have got the hang of it.'

They were out on the veranda, finishing off a delicious alfresco lunch and enjoying the cool thread of a breeze that blew up from the sea. Olinda looked across at him with a rueful smile. 'I wish I could do it as well as you. You really make it look so easy.'

'Don't be so impatient.' Guy winked across at her. 'Remember, I've been doing it for years. I've been skiing and water-skiing almost since I could walk.'

'I suppose you have.' Olinda held his eyes, as, in a flash, she remembered that conversation at the night club when Babette had started off enquiring about his ski chalet and ended up hinting at some related scandal. At the time Olinda had wondered if this might be the story she was seeking, only very rapidly to talk herself out of pursuing it. Now she had the same thought again, but this time with a very different motive.

There would be something rather neat and satisfying, she decided, about using the same lead she had once thought of employing against him to prove now instead that he had no case to answer. If indeed, as Babette had suggested, there had been some scandal, surely his part in it had been innocent? And if that were the case, she thought with a lift, she would be prepared to accept that as her final proof.

She felt a quickening of excitement in her bosom. If she could just get to the bottom of this story, her torment, finally, would be over. And this is your chance, so don't blow it, she warned herself. Go for it! Finally uncover the truth!

She took a deep breath and, sounding casual, proceeded to steer the conversation in the direction she wanted. 'You're very lucky having all these marvellous opportunities to indulge in sports. I suppose in Corsica you water-ski more or less all the year round? And having your own Alpine chalet in the Haute Savoie, you can ski all winter to your heart's content.' She smiled at him and leaned conspiratorially across the table. 'Tell me about your chalet in the Alps. It really does sound quite idyllic.'

Blue eyes smiled back at her. 'It pretty well is. It's in a perfect location, just above two thousand metres. We get the best of the snow and the scenery is fantastic.'

'I'll bet it is—I can just imagine. I'll bet all your friends are clamouring to use it.'

Guy shrugged a small shrug. 'It's pretty popular— and fortunately it's big enough to accommodate a few guests.'

Olinda held her breath for a second, then put to him, smiling, 'I suppose you have lots of parties?'

He met her eyes levelly, still smiling back at her. 'Not a lot. The occasional one or two.'

'That must be fun.' Her heart was beating wildly. She was so close now. She mustn't blow it. Composing her face carefully, her tone studiedly light-hearted, she put to him, 'I suppose sometimes they get a little wild?'

He raised one black eyebrow and laid down his wine glass. 'And why do you suppose that?' he enquired.

Olinda felt her heart give an anxious little squeeze. There was the faintest note of rebuke in his voice, similar to last night when she had quizzed him about his family. But now she was determined to press ahead. This was her golden opportunity.

She threw him an appealing look and confessed to harmless curiosity. 'Babette mentioned something about some wild party involving some prominent minister's wife.' Her grey eyes radiated sympathetic understanding. 'I'm sure it was nothing as scandalous as she made out, but I couldn't help wondering what it was all about.'

There was a pause. Guy looked her straight in the eye. 'Perhaps it was even worse than Babette made out. Or could have been.' His gaze never flickered. 'There was almost a quite enormous scandal, but fortunately it was hushed up in time.'

'Hushed up?' Olinda laughed nervously. She really was on to something! 'It must have been serious, if it had to be hushed up. What on earth was it all about?'

Guy glanced away, his eyes on his wine glass. 'It was not a pretty story. I think it's best forgotten.'

But she had come to the brink now and she could not step back, although it was suddenly a real effort to keep her tone light as she continued to press him. 'Why are you being so secretive?' she teased. 'Go on, tell me about it. I won't tell a soul.'

'You really want to know?' His eyes snapped up to her face, and just for a second, as Olinda looked into them, something inside her told her to say no. But instead she nodded, and then it was too late.

'OK, if you really want to know, I'll tell you.' He leaned towards her and rested his arms on the table-top. 'I've never told anyone any of this before. Perhaps it won't be a bad thing to get it out in the open.' Then, as she swallowed drily, he went on to advise her, 'Though, as I've already warned you, it's not a pretty story.' He paused for a moment. 'Are you sure you want to know?'

Almost mechanically, Olinda nodded. 'Yes,' she murmured, although she was not sure at all.

'OK, here goes.' Guy leaned back in his chair. 'The lady at the centre of the story, the wife of the minister, was a close friend of mine.' His eyes held hers for a flickering moment, so that she was left in no doubt as to what he meant by that. Then, in an oddly flat tone, almost a monotone, he continued, still holding her eyes, 'We were staying at the chalet, secretly, of course—her husband was unaware of our relationship—and one evening there was a party. . .'

Guy paused for a moment, as though to ensure that she was listening, then in the same flat tone he carried on, 'Unfortunately, when the party was at its height, the police turned up, uninvited, and certain substances were discovered. We made the mistake of trying to bribe the police and the whole thing threatened to blow up into a major scandal. Luckily for all of us, because the minister's career was on the line, someone in high office intervened and no charges were brought and the story was smothered.'

He leaned back in his seat and smiled a grim smile. 'It was the closest shave I've ever had in my life. It might very well have been the end of my career if that wretched business had gone to court.'

Olinda looked back at him, feeling dazed and shell-shocked, seeing him suddenly as a stranger. She had her story, she had her proof, but it was not the proof that she'd been looking for.

And suddenly she would have given every penny she owned never to have heard one single word of it.

*   *   *

Of course that was the end of all her illusions. Sickened and shaken by the depravity of Guy's confession, that very same evening, before going to bed, Olinda locked herself in the bathroom and scribbled furiously for half an hour. There could no longer be any doubt as to where her duty lay. What she had just learned she intended passing on to the *Bugle*.

That night she lay wide-eyed and sleepless in her bed, listening to Guy's easy breathing from the mattress on the floor. The man's soul was as savoury as a puddle in a pigsty, yet he had no more conscience than a strip of streaky bacon! She blinked back tears of shame and anger and frustration. With his charm he had tricked her, just as he had tricked Dolores, and not only had she believed in him, she had *wanted* to believe in him, Perhaps that was the most galling part of all.

It was also the part that was more difficult to shake off. For in spite of the letter to Aurora in her bag, all ready to be posted off at the first opportunity, next morning there was still a small corner of her brain that would have welcomed some sign that he was not really so bad. Alas, however, all the signs were to the contrary.

They had arranged to meet Babette and Mel early that morning. The fishing boat was booked for nine o'clock and they were to set off from the marina of their friends' hotel.

'Bring a hamper of food with you,' Babette had advised when they had phoned up to sort out the arrangements. 'Just some chicken legs and some sandwiches, and maybe a bottle of wine.'

Marilyn, the maid, had been charged by Guy with

the responsibility of preparing the hamper and, shortly before eight, as they were getting ready to leave, the good woman brought it out to the car.

'I'll put it in the boot. Give it me here.' With an impatient gesture Guy held out his hand. Then, as Marilyn did as she was bade, he snatched the wicker hamper almost roughly from her hand.

Watching the scene, Olinda winced. It was unlike Guy to behave so rudely—normally he was a personification of good manners—but she had noticed he had seemed oddly edgy today. And, by the looks of things, his edginess was increasing.

Instead of putting the hamper straight into the boot, very pointedly, Guy opened up the lid. His expression curled instantly into angry intolerance. 'What the hell is this supposed to be?' he snapped angrily. 'I told you to pack the white wine, not the red! Stupid bloody woman! Can't you do anything right?'

Olinda watched in shock as Marilyn's face crumpled. 'I'm sorry, sir,' she began. 'I thought——'

'You thought, you thought! Don't tell me what you thought! Just do what I tell you! You're not paid to think!'

It was a disgraceful, unforgivable exhibition and if she had been feeling less vulnerable Olinda would almost certainly have intervened. As it was, she simply turned away, sick and disgusted to her stomach. If she'd had fleeting second thoughts about what she had to do, that unkind little display had firmly put paid to them.

Once they were in the car, she lost no time in asking him, 'Would you mind stopping off at the post office on the way so I can post these extra postcards I've got?'

He didn't even look at her. 'I'm sorry, we haven't time. You can stop off and post them on the way back.'

'It would only take a couple of minutes. I'd really rather post them now.'

'What's so urgent about a couple of postcards?' He turned then to look at her with impatient hard eyes. 'Is there any particular reason why they have to go now?'

'No reason at all.' Olinda clutched her bag guiltily, half afraid that he might suddenly develop X-ray vision and see right through the leather to the telltale envelope that she was anxious to offload as quickly as possible. She forced a bland smile. 'Of course there's no hurry. They can just as easily go this afternoon, if you insist.'

But the postponement, in fact, was a little worrying. Carrying that letter around with her all day would be like walking around with a time-bomb! But there was nothing for it, she decided philosophically. If she were to argue further it would simply make him suspicious, and he was already in a difficult and dangerous enough mood.

Fortunately, his black mood seemed to soften once they were out on the high seas with their friends, and, in spite of its somewhat shaky beginning, the day unfolded remarkably well. Babette and Mel were excellent companions, and the fishing itself, though they caught very little, was an entertaining way of passing the time.

The master of the powerful little boat, a local fisherman named Jaydee, had taken them round to the other side of the island, to the more sombre dark waters of the Atlantic. 'Plenty of barracuda around here,' he promised. 'Maybe you get lucky and catch yourself some!'

Olinda grimaced across at the blonde Babette as the two of them stretched out in the sun, both far more interested in catching a suntan than any such ferocious-sounding prey.

'They never grow up, do they?' laughed Babette, glancing fondly across at her husband. 'No matter how old they are they're always little boys at heart.'

Olinda pushed back the strands of light brown hair that the warm wind had whipped across her face and let her eyes drift round to the stern of the boat and the dark-haired figure in the brief khaki shorts who was sitting with his back to her. As he sat there in the bolted-in, swivel fishing seat, wielding the heavy rod like an expert, he did have a faintly boyish air about him that to an innocent onlooker might have seemed disarming. But as she smiled back at Babette in tacit agreement, Olinda felt only a sense of deep disappointment. It was sad that so physically fine a man should in all other respects be so base and shallow. If only his façade of decency were real, he would come dangerously close to male perfection.

It was a short while later that Jaydee called for a break. 'The four of you can have lunch,' he told them, 'while I take us out into deeper waters.'

It was a timely break. As the two eager couples gathered round their hampers, it was clear that the sea air had sharpened their appetites.

Guy pulled out some Creole-cooked chicken legs from a napkin and kissed his fingertips in French-style appreciation. '*Formidable!*' he pronounced with enthusiasm, urging Babette and Mel to help themselves. 'These look absoluely delicious!'

From beneath her lashes Olinda threw him a look of disapproval, remembering the scene over the bottle of wine. Why had he been so unkind to Marilyn when she did such an excellent job of looking after them? But in his typically arrogant and capricious fashion he appeared completely to have forgotten that nasty little episode, as he uncorked the bottle and poured the wine into glasses and, with a bone-melting smile, passed the first one to Olinda.

'*Santé, chérie!*' He held his own glass out to her, inviting her to join him in a toast. Then, as their glasses touched, he reached out affectionately to draw her towards him for a brief kiss.

Olinda hated the way her senses flared within her at the delicate, sensual brush of his lips. How could her flesh be so hopelessly fickle when she had turned her heart so implacably against him? She felt a sudden urgency for this holiday to be over. After all, she had her story. She no longer needed him. And every minute she was forced to spend with him, from now on, would be a penance.

Babette, however, had read the situation rather differently. When, later, the men resumed their fishing and the two women once more lay stretched out in the sun, Babette glanced across at Olinda and confided with a smile, 'If I weren't a happily married woman, I would envy you, you know. The two of you look so good together. Make sure you hang on to him. He's a man in a million.'

Poor, deluded Babette. Olinda smiled back thinly. 'I don't think either of us are really that serious about one another. It's nothing more than a holiday romance.'

Babette raised an eyebrow. 'That's a pity.' Then she smiled wryly as she shook back her short blonde hair. 'I used to have high hopes of me and Guy,' she confessed, 'but I guess I met him at the wrong time. It was just shortly after his father died and he took over the running of the Foundation. I'm afraid he had rather a lot on his mind.'

Olinda looked surprised. 'You've known him that long? I'd no idea you were such long-standing friends.'

Babette smiled. 'Eight years or so. Yes, I suppose it is rather a long time.'

Eight years or so? That couldn't be right. 'But surely he took over the company when he was just twenty-one? That was all of *fifteen* years ago!'

Babette was shaking her head and laughing. 'You've got your facts a little wrong, I'm afraid. He was young when he took over, but not *that* young. He was nearly twenty-eight.'

Olinda frowned in confusion. How very peculiar. It was Dolores who had told her he had been just twenty-one. Had she lied about that too, or made a genuine mistake?

But Olinda had no time to ponder that mystery further, for it was at that very moment that Mel let out a cry of triumph.

'Hey, you guys, I've got a bite!'

Instantly Jaydee was there beside him. 'It feels like a big one. You'd better put on the harness.' With a nod of his head he indicated the leather safety harness that was attached to Mel's swivel seat. 'Some of these dudes are mighty strong. They can put up a helluva fight.'

But, ignoring the danger he might be in, Mel turned with a grin to share his elation with his wife, momentarily slackening his grip on the rod as he did so.

It was only a moment, but it was enough. An instant later, to Olinda's horror, the fishing line tautened with a vicious jerk, snapping Mel from his seat as though he were a puppet and dragging him, slithering, across the deck. No harm would have come to him if he had let go of the rod, as Jaydee was yelling at him to do, but with grim determination he continued to clutch on to it as the force of the line drag slammed him against the side of the boat.

Already Guy was on his feet, his arm snatching out to grab at his friend. But his reach was a millimetre short and a moment later, in horrific slow motion, Mel was catapulted over the side of the boat.

There was an instant of silence, like time suspended, when the four figures on board seemed to freeze in their tracks. Then, in the blink of an eyelid, before the others recovered, Guy was vaulting easily on to the guard rail and diving into the ocean after his friend.

Even before she heard the splash, as he cut cleanly through the churning grey waters, Olinda was staggering in alarm to her feet, her heart leaping anxiously to her throat. She looked at Babette, who looked right back at her, and, without the need to utter one single syllable, each knew instantly what the other was thinking. It was written in the stark fear that shone from their faces. A single, terrifying word.

Barracuda.

As Jaydee raced to the controls to slow the boat down, at the same time instructing, 'Grab the lifebelts!' like two panic-stricken automatons, Olinda and Babette were hurling themselves towards the stern of the boat. Olinda got there first and leaned over the guard rail, her heart sick within her, as she gazed down into the waves.

There was no sign of either man. Not a ripple. It was as though they had both been instantly snatched away and silently swallowed into the deep.

'Oh, my God! Dear God, have mercy,' Olinda was praying under her breath, feeling a wave of terror, icy cold, slowly rise up from the soles of her feet. In an instant it had engulfed her, paralysing her brain and numbing her senses. Every emotion seemed to have died inside her, every emotion save a stark, colossal fear.

'Look out to starboard!'

As Jaydee shouted, Olinda swung round to follow with her eyes his pointing finger. And there, about fifty yards from the boat, a dark head was bobbing to the surface. For the faintest fraction of a second, her stomach unclenched in giddy relief. It was Guy, and he was waving towards them. She could scarcely believe it. The sea had not claimed him!

A moment later a second head appeared—though she could tell at a glance that Mel was unconscious, his limp body supported in Guy's strong arms. Then Jaydee was at the guard rail, grabbing one of the lifebelts and flinging it over the side towards the two men. At once Guy was swimming strongly towards it, still supporting

Mel with one arm, and Jaydee was quickly pulling them in to the side of the boat, and safety.

What seemed like an endless eternity later, but in reality was no more than a couple of minutes, Mel was being dragged over the side of the boat, to be followed by the broad-shouldered form of Guy, lifting himself easily down on to the deck.

Paralysed with emotion, Olinda stood and stared at him, as though her feet were nailed to the deck, taking in the fact that he was, mercifully, unharmed and that she had never felt more ecstatic about anything in her life. Then, as he looked at her with that half-smile she had grown so used to, something inside her seemed to break free and she was flinging herself across the deck towards him, her heart stopping as he swung her up into his arms.

As he gathered her to him, her arms were round his neck, her face buried against his, weeping tears of relief. 'Oh, thank God you're safe,' she heard herself sobbing, as she stroked his dark hair with quivering hands. 'Don't ever do anything like that again! I would die if anything were ever to happen to you!'

For the next half-hour or so everyone's attention was focused on the shocked, prone form of Mel.

Once on board he recovered consciousness quickly, but he was still dazed and in a state of shock. Jaydee gave them blankets to wrap around him, as they laid him down in the cabin and made him drink cups of sweet, hot coffee.

'I'm fine now. Don't worry about me,' Mel insisted, clearly embarrassed by the upset he had caused. 'I'm just sorry I was such a careless idiot and ended up putting Guy in danger as well.'

Guy was modest and reassuring. 'Accidents can happen to anyone,' he insisted. 'Maybe one day you'll do the same for me.'

Of course, it was the end of the fishing expedition. No one was quite in the mood any more. So, on Guy's instructions, Jaydee turned the boat around and headed back towards Barbados.

It was still relatively early—just after five—when they docked at the marina of Babette and Mel's hotel. 'Stay and have a drink with us before you go back to your villa,' Babette tried to insist.

But Guy was adamant. 'Mel needs to rest. Both of you do, as a matter of fact. You've just had an exceedingly nasty shock.' He touched Babette's arm in a kind, supportive gesture. 'Don't worry, we'll see you again before we leave.'

And so, just as twilight was rapidly gathering—night fell quickly here in the tropics—Guy and Olinda climbed into the Cadillac and started to head back to Silver Cove.

A strange mood had settled on Olinda once that moment of abandon on the boat had passed. And though she had tried to drive the memory of it from her, even privately deny it had ever occurred, those few vivid moments, and all the emotions that had torn through her, were tattooed in bright colours across her brain.

As she had clung to him, sliding her hands through his hair and pressing warm kisses against his neck, for one startling moment that would never leave her she had been filled with a sense of total bliss. For in that moment of what had felt like divine revelation, she had believed, totally and unreservedly, that she loved him.

It was a quite appalling thought, yet in that heady instant her heart had lit up like a Roman candle. Quite unable to resist the emotions that enthralled her, she had poured out her passion on a torrent of sweet kisses, all the while filled with a rash, desperate longing to put her adoration into words.

And she had said too much. The memory of the words she had spoken shamed her. But at least she hadn't said the most damning words of all. She had not spoken the words 'I love you'.

Be grateful for small mercies, she told herself grimly. As it was, she had betrayed herself badly enough. It seemed her heart had no sense and no decency. How could it be so base as to love such a man?

As they drove now along the coast road towards the villa, Olinda was dreading the thought of being alone with Guy. She could just imagine how cynically he would respond now to that shamelessly unbridled display of emotion. But if he had any ideas about cashing in on it, she would very quickly put him right about that.

His tone, however, revealed nothing of what he was thinking, as he suddenly turned to her and said, 'Hey, aren't we forgetting something? We'd better get to the post office before it closes.'

Olinda frowned blankly. 'The post office? What for?' For an instant she hadn't a clue what he was talking about.

'Your postcards,' he reminded her, slanting a glance

across at her. 'The ones you were so anxious to post this morning.'

'Oh, yes—of course.' Now she remembered what all the recent emotional upheaval had driven from her mind. The letter she had written to the *Bugle* that was still ticking like a time-bomb in her bag. 'I'd forgotten all about them,' she offered, smiling weakly. And her fingers tightened involuntarily around her bag, as a sudden shaft of cold apprehension drove through her.

Guy was continuing to watch her, one dark eyebrow lifted. 'You still want to post them, I take it?' he said.

She met his eyes and then glanced away hurriedly. 'Oh, yes,' she assured him. 'Of course I do.'

Outside the post office Guy pulled on the handbrake. 'I'll wait here in the car,' he told her. 'You go off and do what you have to do.'

It was only as she stepped out on to the pavement that Olinda was assailed by a sudden flood of doubts. All at once what she was about to do seemed a little unsavoury. She felt a stab of conscience as she stepped away from the car.

For how could she so cold-bloodedly betray the man who, only a few short hours ago, she had come to believe she loved?

Because she did not, because she *could* not love him, she argued, and by posting the letter she would prove that.

She stepped decisively through the main door of the post office and joined the short queue of customers waiting to be served. Think of Dolores, think of Marilyn, think of that story he told you last night! The man isn't worth your crazy feelings, she argued. Show a little backbone. Treat him as he deserves!

But as her turn at the counter came all too quickly, the doubts were multiplying inside her head. There were so many things that just didn't add up, an ever-growing mass of confusing imponderables. Like that story of Babette's today that just didn't tally with Dolores' version—all of which, in turn reminded her of that highly suspect tale about the opera.

As the counter clerk glanced up at her—'How can I help you, miss?'—Olinda was almost weeping with frustration. Was she simply looking for ways out again, allowing her good sense to fall hostage to her emotions?

The counter clerk was waiting and there were people behind her. As she stood there in stricken silence she was holding up the line. She took a deep breath. 'I want some stamps, please.' Then in a flash of inspiration, she made up her mind. She would not, after all, post the letter today. She would sleep on the problem and maybe post it tomorrow.

'Stamps for England,' she elaborated, smiling. Then, with a sense of relief that the decision was taken, she reached into her bag for her few postcards, and instantly felt the blood in her veins freeze solid. For the letter she had so agonised about was no longer there.

The shock of the discovery was like a body blow to her senses. How could it be? Where had the letter gone? Numb with trepidation, she paid for her stamps and somehow managed to stick them on her postcards. It must have fallen out while she was on the boat, or perhaps later at Babette and Mel's hotel.

In a kind of agony her mind went over all the

possibilities, struggling to remember every instance when she had removed or replaced anything in her bag. But it was a hopeless, thankless, pointless exercise. The letter had gone, and that was that.

She stepped out of the post office and into the street, feeling chilled and shivery despite the warm air. If she had dropped it at the hotel, that was not so serious, for there was nothing on the envelope to connect it with her. But if Jaydee were to discover it on his boat, he would know it belonged to one of today's passengers and would presumably contact Babette and Mel. They in turn would rightly assume that it was either the property of Guy or herself.

She arrived at the car, her heart like lead in her chest, and, as Guy pushed open the passenger door, climbed distractedly inside.

'Did you get everything done?' he was enquiring pleasantly, glancing quickly across at her, as he switched on the engine.

'Yes, thanks,' she nodded without looking at him. Suddenly she felt like bursting into tears.

On the journey back, locked in her own private panic, Olinda was immensely grateful that Guy, for once, made no attempt at conversation. She would have been incapable of putting two words together. Every corner of her brain was suddenly focused on the horror that was bound to ensue if the nature of that letter were ever uncovered.

She quailed at the thought, quite literally terrified. If Guy were to discover what she had been up to, her poor wretched life would not be worth living. His anger, and his vengeance, would surely be terrible.

So she must think of a way to avoid such calamity. For there must be a way, if her brain could but devise it.

As they swung through the big iron gates of the villa and headed swiftly up the driveway, her grey cells were churning with demented fury. She pushed open the car door and stepped on to the gravel, suddenly desperate to be by herself. If she could just have an hour of peace and tranquillity, perhaps she could come up with some idea that, possibly, might still save her.

But as she hurried up the staircase to the veranda, suddenly Guy was right behind her. 'Where are you off to?' he demanded softly, snatching her lightly by the wrist. 'You seem to be in a bit of a rush.'

With a catch of impatience, she turned to glare down at him. 'I'm going to have a bath,' she snapped. 'A long, relaxing bath.'

'Good idea.' But he did not release her. And his eyes were suddenly as hard as sapphires, as his free hand reached round to the back pocket of his trousers and in one quick movement drew something out. The hand around her wrist had tightened ferociously. 'You may have your bath, *chérie*,' he ground at her menacingly, 'just as soon as you and I have had a chance to talk.'

'Talk? About what?' She was still trying to free herself.

But a moment later she stiffened in horror as, in a tone that chilled her to her very marrow, he enlightened her carefully, 'About this, *chérie*.'

And with a flourish he held up before her disbelieving gaze, crumpled and torn open, the missing letter.

CHAPTER EIGHT

OLINDA stared at the letter in stunned disbelief. 'You. . .!' she stammered, feeling the blood drain out of her. 'Where on earth did you find that?'

By way of an answer Guy twisted her arm sharply and started to march her up the wooden staircase. At the top he flung her bodily into the drawing-room, so that she staggered and fell into one of the armchairs. 'I found it in your bag,' he gritted, standing over her. 'And I read it while you were in the post office, supposedly buying stamps for your postcards!'

Olinda suddenly felt as though she had stumbled headlong into a nightmare. As she slumped like a rag doll against the cushions, the palms of her fists were clammy and damp, and the beads of cold sweat that glistened on her forehead had nothing whatsoever to do with the heat.

Feebly she demanded, 'And what right have you to go raking in my bag and reading my private correspondence?' It was a pathetic attempt at self-defence, but it was all her suddenly paralysed brain could come up with.

Guy let out a snarl that curdled her blood and caused her to shrink back in her chair. 'You dare to demand what right have *I*?' The blue fire of fury flashed from his eyes. 'It is not I, *chérie*, who am under interrogation! *You* are the one who has some explaining to do!'

His anger was so real and so vivid that it felt like a third person in the room. And he looked as though he might devour her, as he stood there, towering threateningly over her, a dark and dangerously menacing figure in light cotton trousers and body-hugging T-shirt. Olinda drew her legs up beneath the skirt of her sundress and struggled to meet the fury in his eyes. 'I wan't going to send it,' she offered in sheer misery. 'I swear I wasn't. I'd changed my mind.'

'I'll bet you had!' He did not believe her. His lips curled in an expression of harsh disdain. Then he took a step closer, as though to grab hold of her, and the dark brows knitted into a scowl. 'What I want to know is *why* you were doing it!' he gritted. He stooped down abruptly to grab her by the arm, thrusting his furious face into hers. 'Who the hell are you, anyway?' he demanded.

The tension inside her tightened like a noose. Olinda swallowed. 'Who am I?' she babbled.

'Who are you, *ma chérie*? A simple enough question!' The muscles of the dark jaw clenched with impatience, as he thrust his face even closer to hers. His eyes drove into her like skewers. 'Will you answer—or do I have to force it out of you?'

Olinda opened her mouth, but no words came. Her brain all at once was incapable of forming any, and her heart was hammering so loudly in her chest that she was scarcely able to hear herself think.

'I asked you a question! I'm waiting for an answer!' His face was livid with barely controlled anger, as his free hand suddenly grabbed her by the throat. Fingers like steel wire closed around her, making her jerk back in panic and gasp for breath. 'I'm waiting for you to tell me who you are!'

Her hands flew up to prise his fingers away, as her head was slammed against the back of the chair. But she had the strength of a flea compared to the power that held her. As she struggled, he merely tightened his grip.

'Spit it out, *chérie*! Who the hell are you?'

She could scarcely breathe, though it was her fear that was choking her, rather than the hand that held her captive. She closed her eyes, not daring to look at him. 'I'm Dolores' sister,' she murmured finally.

For a moment a stillness and a silence descended, as though he was digesting what she had just said. Then, as her eyes fluttered open, Guy demanded slowly, 'You mean Dolores Reid? My ex-secretary who died?'

His fingers around her throat had slackened. Olinda nodded. 'Yes. So you do remember her?'

'Of course I remember her!' His tone was impatient, as at last he released her and stepped away. 'But I don't understand why Dolores' sister should be involved in a deliberate campaign to destroy me.' The blue eyes narrowed, glinting coldly. 'I take it that is what you were trying to do?'

She felt a wash of cold shame for the depth of her deception. After all, he had trusted her and she had betrayed him. Then she thrust her shame away. He deserved it! And, looking back at him steadily, she told him, 'I wanted to pay you back for Dolores' death.'

'Dolores' death?' Guy frowned, perplexed. 'What had Dolores' death to do with me? She died by her own hand, as I understand it, nearly a year after she returned to England.'

'Thanks to you and what you did to her!' The accusation tripped easily from her tongue. She had believed it for so long now that it came without thinking. Yet, deep within her, uncertainty was growing. The truth was she was no longer one hundred per cent sure.

He stood before her, very still. 'And what did I do to her?' he demanded.

'You broke her heart, that's what you did! You may not have been there when she died, but it was you who drove her to take her own life!'

'I doubt that very much indeed.' His tone was scathing, almost callous. 'If not me, then someone or something else would eventually have driven her over the edge. Your sister, as you must have known, was emotionally unstable. She already had a divorce and a string of broken relationships behind her before she ever encountered me.'

Sudden anger flared within Olinda. He was defending himself by slandering Dolores! 'My sister was not emotionally unstable! She was simply unlucky, a bad judge of men.' Her eyes narrowed accusingly. 'And, since you say you were aware of her background, wasn't that all the more reason to treat her with a bit of compassion and consideration? Or does a man like you simply regard a vulnerable woman as a piece of easy game?'

He did not answer, but his silence was thunderous. It filled the room with such terrible menace that Olinda quickly hurried on,

'Why couldn't you have just left her alone if you didn't want her? Why did you have to lead her on?'

The blue eyes narrowed. 'Is that what she told you?'

'Do you deny it?'

'Damned right I deny it!'

He had turned away, abruptly, to look out on to the veranda, his broad back presented to the armchair where she sat. Olinda rose unsteadily to her feet, afraid that he might decide to terminate the conversation and walk out on her before she had finished. For, in spite of the bitter attack she was launching, one anguished part of her was longing for the denial that would finally demolish all that she had previously believed.

Her voice was unsteady as she demanded, 'Are you saying that you never made her any promises, that you never proposed marriage, that she invented all of it?'

He swung round to look at her. 'Quite emphatically I deny it! The very idea is preposterous!'

Olinda's heart flickered. She clenched her fists tightly. 'Can you prove it?' she demanded.

'Prove it?' Suddenly he was standing over her again. In two angry strides he had closed the gap between them. 'If anyone needs to prove anything, it's you, not me!' He snatched the letter once more from his pocket and thrust it angrily in front of her face. 'You're the one who's making accusations. The onus of proof lies with you, *chérie*!'

Suddenly his hand was on her shoulder, his grip as cruel and relentless as a vice. 'So what other little snippets have you passed on to the *Bugle*? Come on, out with it! What else have you told them?'

Olinda winced beneath the steel of his fingers. 'Only

that you drove my sister to her death. Nothing else, I swear! Only that.'

'You told them that?' He let loose an oath. 'My God, you've really had a field day!' His fingers dug into her shoulder like pincers. 'So tell me, *chérie*, when did you plan all this? Did you come to the conference with your plan all prepared?'

'Of course I didn't! I didn't even know you'd be there! I only really decided to do it when you told me about those people who were after you and forced me to take part in this stupid charade.'

The blue eyes narrowed disbelievingly. 'So why did you steal my tape recorder?'

Olinda looked back at him miserably. She had almost forgotten that stupid gesture that had been the fatal beginning that had led to all this mess. 'That had nothing to do with this. I just took it to inconvenience you. I hadn't even thought of any of the other stuff at that point. Please believe me. It was you yourself who gave me the idea!'

'I see.' Apparently, thank heaven, he believed her. He released her shoulder and let his hand drop away. 'So, after I so generously gave you the idea, you decided to get in touch with this woman at the *Bugle* and offer your services as informer? If the other lot didn't nail me, then you would?'

'Something like that,' she admitted uneasily. The way he had put it it sounded nasty and crude.

He stepped back slowly and surveyed her. 'You know, it's all just starting to come back to me—Lulu.' As she blanched at the mention of her old childish name, Guy smiled a wryly bitter smile. 'Whoever would have thought that that innocent young kid who I met all those years ago on Corsica would turn into such a vicious and deceitful specimen? Playing the double agent, no less. You must be feeling pretty proud of yourself!'

As a matter of fact that was far from the truth. Olinda felt cheap and grubby and profoundly ashamed of herself. 'I wasn't going to send the letter,' she protested. 'I told you before, I'd changed my mind.'

'Of course you had!' Guy mimicked understanding. 'That's why you were so keen for me to drive you to the post office.' Then in a deliberately vicious gesture he flung the letter at her, so that it collided momentarily with her shoulder, then fluttered ignominiously to the floor. 'But I'm afraid, *ma chère*, you'll never make a spy. It was the way you kept asking me leading questions that made me suspect that you might be up to something—though I confess, it never crossed my mind that it would be something as nasty and devious as this.'

He paused and raked her face with eyes like steel hooks. 'By the way, the story I gave you was sheer invention, invented to satisfy your curiosity. That whole nasty episode did in fact happen, and more or less as I related it, but I was not involved and it did not take place at my chalet.' He laughed harshly, without humour. 'Check it out if you like. Or send it to your friends at the *Bugle* and have them check it out for you!'

He punched his fists into the pockets of his trousers, as though the better to keep them under control, and regarded her as one might regard a stain on the carpet.

'I thought your sister was a bare-faced liar, but you are in a class all of your own!'

Then, as though he could no longer bear to breathe the same air as her, he turned away contemptuously and strode out of the room. Olinda heard his footsteps clatter down the staircase, then a minute later the car crunched off down the drive.

After he had gone she sat for a long time, staring blankly at the letter in her hand. What a fool she had been to believe she could best him! He had had the measure of her more or less right from the start!

In a gesture of impatience she crumpled the letter and flung it with all her strength across the room. She had no need to check whether the story was false, for she knew beyond a shred of doubt that it was.

In spite of his faults, Guy was no low-life character, to have been involved in such a sordid affair. Had she only stopped to think about it rationally for a moment, she would surely have realised that for herself. As it was, from the very first moment she had heard it, the story had troubled her more than it had pleased her, and now it was an enormous relief to have it formally denied.

She grimaced to herself. What an idiot she would have looked if she'd gone ahead and sent the story to the *Bugle*! At the very least, after checking it out, they would have dismissed her as some kind of malicious crank!

She ran her fingers through her tangled brown hair. So what now of Guy's guilt regarding Dolores? Had she finally been proved wrong about that as well?

Wearily she leaned against the cushions, remembering his angry, dismissive response to her request that he supply her with proof of his innocence. 'The onus of proof lies with you, *chérie*! You're the one who's making accusations!'

He was right, of course, and what proof did she have, apart from the discredited word of her sister? Although a couple of lies were by no means proof that Dolores had invented her entire story, they surely had to cast serious doubts. It was no longer just a case, Olinda realised with mixed feelings, of her trying to justify her own guilt-ridden emotions. Regardless of what she might feel for Guy, she could no longer decently continue to accuse him.

And in that case, she realised with sudden certainty, there was only one thing left for her to do.

Decisively, she rose from her chair and crossed to the telephone out in the hall. She picked up the receiver and dialled for the operator. 'Hello? I want to send an international telegram.'

A few minutes later, as she laid down the receiver, she felt as though an enormous burden had been lifted from her shoulders. The telegram had been addressed to Miss Benjamin at the *Bugle*, retracting every word of her original story about Guy and Dolores and stating, finally and unequivocally, that she would no longer be supplying information against Guy.

She went out on to the veranda and crossed to the parapet, feeling drained of emotion and weary to her bones. As soon as Guy returned, she would tell him about the telegram and just pray that he could find it in his heart to forgive her.

With a bleak inner sigh she leaned against the parapet and gazed up at the star-crowded sky. The way she had betrayed him was unspeakable, and it was more than likely now that he hated her. Yet perhaps, if he were to see that she was truly repentant, he might allow her a second chance.

A second chance for what? she asked herself wearily. To try to redeem whatever hope they might have had of forming some kind of meaningful relationship? There had been scant hope of that from the very beginning. What possible hope could there be now?

As despair tore through her she gazed up at the sky. Why did fate have to treat her so cruelly again? Had Julian just been a taster for this far, far greater heart-break? Had destiny planted this love within her only in order that it might torture her?

She frowned at the moon that hung on the horizon, as though it might offer her some answers. But the huge silver sphere had no solace to offer. It just shone back at her, cold and aloof and uncaring. If there were answers to be had, it was she who must find them.

Next morning Guy was still mysteriously absent.

Just after eight Olinda trudged through to breakfast, feeling racked and weary after a night without sleeping, waiting on tenterhooks for his return. As she picked up her papaya, she could feel Marilyn watching her, discreetly, from the corner of her eye. 'I don't suppose you've had any word from Mr de Chevalley?' she finally forced herself to ask, hoping that she had managed to sound casual, in spite of the revealing nature of her enquiry.

'No, miss, I ain't heard nothing.' As Marilyn met her eyes, she seemed to pause for a moment, as though considering the wisdom of confiding more. Then, suddenly decisive, she wiped her hands on her apron and came across the veranda to stand before Olinda. 'I can see you're worried, so I reckon it's time I told you.' Without bothering to wait for an invitation, she pulled out a chair and promptly sat down. 'That man of yours is up to something—and there's something I think you maybe ought to know.'

Olinda straightened, disguising the foolish flutter she had felt at hearing Guy described as her man. However misguided Marilyn's perception of their relationship, it was obvious that the woman knew something she didn't. 'Tell me,' she demanded, suddenly attentive.

'Well. . .' Marilyn smoothed her apron over her plump knees. 'I ought to explain about yesterday morning, for a start. That little argy-bargy about the wine, when Mr Guy really laid into me. . .' To Olinda's surprise, her face broke into a smile. 'I don't know if you realised it, but that was all an act.'

Taken aback, Olinda blinked at her. 'You mean it was staged? But what on earth for?'

Marilyn shrugged. 'I'm not sure, miss. He didn't tell me any details. All he told me was that he thought there were some people watching the house and that if we could make them think there was bad blood between us, they might very likely come knocking on the door, persuading me to get my own back by spying on you and Mr Guy and passing on any bits of scandal I knew.' Her face sobered, as she assured her enraptured listener, 'Of course, I would never do a thing like that.

That would be downright disloyal on my part. But Mr Guy told me what to tell them, if he turned out to be right and they did show up.'

'And did they?' Olinda wanted to know. 'Did anyone come knocking on the door?'

'Sure enough they did. While you were out fishing. A red-haired woman and a skinny young man.'

The same pair from the Humming Bird Club that Guy had told her he had spotted that night! 'And what did he tell you to tell them?' urged Olinda.

Marilyn sat back, thoroughly enjoying herself. 'Well, Mr Guy had told me to tell them I could sell them something more interesting than a bit of old gossip. Photographs. Secret photographs that Mr Guy kept in the glove compartment of his car.' She gave an appreciative giggle, shaking her head, and Olinda could just imagine how convincingly she had played her part. 'I told them I could get the photographs when I was cleaning the car out when you got back from your fishing trip, and I made an appointment to meet them yesterday evening at a little hotel in Bridgetown to hand them over.'

She pulled a face. 'Of course, they offered me money, but I was never planning to keep the appointment, nor to steal no photographs from the car. Mr Guy said he'd be keeping the appointment in my place—and that, Miss Olinda, is all I know.' She stood up abruptly and smiled down at Olinda. 'Mr Guy told me to keep it to myself, but I figured, with him having disappeared and all, that maybe you ought to know.'

Olinda smiled at her. 'I'm glad you told me.' And she was, indeed, immensely grateful—though not a little irked as well—to have been so belatedly let in on Guy's little secret.

For one thing, it was a relief to have an explanation for his absence, for, secretly, she had been more than a little worried. He had left last evening in such a terrible temper that she had feared that some accident might have befallen him.

It was also quite enormously reassuring to learn that that scene with Marilyn yesterday had merely been another of his staged charades. It had deeply and genuinely disturbed her to believe that he was capable of treating a servant so badly.

She returned to her papaya with a little more appetite and put up a prayer that his mission had succeeded. If he had finally managed to nail his tormentors, then he was likely to return in a more generous mood.

Again, the hope inside her flickered, and, with it, a sobering cold dart of fear. It meant so much to her that he forgive her. She could not bear to think that he might not.

She closed her eyes as the fear grew into a torrent, eddying through her, engulfing her heart. In truth she longed for so much more than his forgiveness, but it would be sheer folly even to hope.

She closed her eyes and squeezed the tears back. Just his forgiveness was what she must aim for. With that alone she must be content.

It was well into the afternoon when Olinda heard the Cadillac come up the driveway. She was out on the veranda, stretched out on a sunbed, trying to read a magazine.

At the sound of crunching tyres, her heart stopped within her. This was it. Her waiting was over. Now she would have her moment of truth.

As the car door slammed and the sound of footsteps started to come up the wooden staircase, she took a deep breath and hurriedly composed herself, pulling a colourful beach robe over her bikini. Then, fighting back her panic, she held her breath and waited, as the footsteps rapidly approached the veranda.

A moment later he was standing before her, a dark, vital figure in light trousers and T-shirt—and just for a fraction of a second her heart lit up with a shaft of pure pleasure for the sheer magical joy of seeing him again.

It was evident that her feelings were not reciprocated. With one look Guy froze the smile on her face. 'So you're still here,' he commented flatly.

With an effort of will she managed to conceal the lance-like pain that went knifing through her. Where else did he expect her to be? Had he perhaps been hoping that she might have left?

Bunching her fists in determination—she would not allow herself to be discouraged by this unfavourable opening!—she forced herself to look into his face and enquired in a gently optimistic tone, 'Marilyn told me you'd gone after these people—the ones who've been following you around. Did you have any joy? Did you manage to catch them?'

Without answering, he leaned against the wooden parapet and slotted his hands into the pockets of his trousers. 'And what if I did?' he demanded curtly. 'Of what possible interest could it be to you?'

He was standing against the sun, so that his features

were in shadow, his head and shoulders in bright silhouette. And Olinda was all at once immensely grateful that she did not have to look into his eyes. The ice-cold condemnation she would see there would surely have withered her very soul. As it was, her insides had shrunk at his words.

'I am interested. Truly,' she insisted. 'I hope you managed to track them down.'

'Are you sure you don't mean you hope I failed? I think you're forgetting which side you're on.'

Olinda swallowed drily. He was being merciless. 'I told you before, I changed my mind. While you were gone I even sent a telegram to the *Bugle*, taking back everything I said against you. *Really*,' she emphasised, as his expression failed to soften. 'I'm telling you the truth. You've got to believe me.'

'And why should I do that?' He gave an abrupt, dismissive laugh. 'Why should I believe someone who has done nothing but deceive me from the very first moment that we met?'

'Because I'm not trying to deceive you any more. I'm trying to make up for what I've done.' Her voice fractured a little, as she added emotionally, 'I swear it on the memory of my dead sister.'

She felt Guy's blue gaze fix on her in the silence that followed. It was an effort not to blink or glance away. Then he spoke at last. 'So what's caused this sudden turnaround—if turnaround it truly is?'

So he was halfway to believing her. She relaxed a little. 'I realised that what you said was right. I don't have any proof of anything. It's simply your word against my sister's.'

He gave a cynical laugh. 'How very touching! I thought the word of your sister was sacrosanct?'

Olinda glanced away to hide her own confusion. Once she had believed that with every fibre of her being, but now the truth was that she no longer even wanted to believe it. Then she deliberately swivelled her gaze back to him. 'I've told you honestly that I'm no longer against you. Why won't you at least give me the benefit of the doubt?'

With a sharp sigh that spoke more of impatience than of capitulation, Guy detached himself from the wooden parapet and paused for a moment before stepping towards her. Then he seated himself in one of the cane chairs opposite her and regarded her with unreadable eyes. 'OK. Since you're so interested, I'll tell you what happened. In spite of your original plan to do the opposite, you undoubtedly contributed to my success.'

Olinda's heart did a funny little shuffle. This was a very definite improvement. Then she leaned towards him, genuinely excited. 'You mean you actually managed to catch them?' she breathed.

Guy nodded. 'It was extremely easy in the end. They were not particularly clever.' He raised one dark eyebrow and digressed briefly, 'By the way, I knew Marilyn would spill the beans about our little plot. She's a good-hearted woman; she wouldn't want to leave you in suspense.'

Olinda glanced away, hardly able to contain the hope that was suddenly flickering within her. So, in spite of the way he had believed she had betrayed him, he had had the generosity to spare a thought for her. Perhaps all was not completely lost. She could only pray that she was right, as he continued with his story.

'Last night, after I left here, I went to keep the appointment that Marilyn had made—at an obscure little hotel in the centre of Bridgetown, where they were expecting to pick up the fictitious set of photos. I went early and booked a room in Marilyn's name and told the desk clerk to tell them when they arrived that Marilyn was waiting for them upstairs.' He allowed himself a triumphant little smile. 'It was a simple enough trap, but they walked straight into it.'

'And was it them?' Olinda was listening intently. 'Was it the couple you saw at the nightclub?'

'It was them all right. A certain Madame Claude Boucher, wife of an ex-employee of mine, and a hired photographer, Emile Lopez.' He shook his head. 'Once they knew they were cornered, they were a pathetic pair—spilled the beans with no bother at all. And the whole sorry story, as it turns out, is more or less as I'd expected.'

He leaned back a little and laid his long, tanned hands along the cane arms of his chair. 'Claude Boucher used to work for the Foundation. He was an admin man and damned good at his job. But unfortunately he was greedy and got himself involved in all sorts of fiddles on the side. He'd made himself quite a little pile before he was finally discovered and publicly fired. Last I heard he'd gone off to Montreal, but apparently he moved south, to Houston, three years ago. In the meantime, he's made a new life for himself, including acquiring a Texan wife.'

Guy smiled a cynical smile and sighed. 'He would have been wise just to have left things as they were, but, sadly for him, he was bent on revenge—he'd never forgiven me for exposing him—and when this takeover controversy landed right in his back yard he just couldn't resist trying to screw things up for me.' He paused to deliver a meaningful smile. 'But revenge has a nasty habit of going wrong. Especially when it's so hopelessly ill-conceived.'

Olinda felt the rebuke like a slap in the face. Hadn't she just learned that bitter lesson for herself?

Abruptly she changed the subject and urged him to continue. 'So this Claude Boucher, you say, was behind it? And he got his wife and this photographer to follow you around——'

'—in the hope of catching me with my trousers down.' As Guy finished the sentence for her, he smiled wryly. 'That's more or less it. In the meantime, he and a couple of his cronies were busily picking over every inch of newsprint that has been published about me over the years, in the hope of digging up something that could damage me. I'm happy to say they'd had no success.'

'So, after they had confessed, what happened next?'

'Well, I was careful to tape the entire confession—unbeknown to them, of course. Then, after I'd forced Boucher's wife to give me their Houston address, I caught the first flight back to the States and went straight to call on Boucher personally. I shall spare you the details of what passed between us. It wasn't particularly pleasant. Suffice it to say that the entire matter has now been placed in the hands of the police.'

He let his hands slide along the arms of his chair and added, on a note of triumph, 'The whole thing has been most satisfactorily concluded—and, into the bargain, on the phone last night I received the news that the takeover has finally been approved.'

Olinda felt a warm glow of happiness for him—and even a measure of redemption for herself. At least her folly had done him no perceptible damage—and that was something to be profoundly grateful for. For if it had, she now realised with startling clarity, she would never have been able to forgive herself. Thank heaven she had proved such a resounding failure in the field of espionage!

She was just about to express these thoughts when Guy shifted his chair and began to stand up. 'So. All's well that ends well, as they say. I reckon we ought to put our differences behind us. There's no point at all in carrying around grudges.'

'Do you really mean it?' Olinda jumped to her feet, scarcely able to believe her ears. 'You mean you forgive me, after all?' she breathed.

A light smile briefly touched his lips and was echoed for an instant in his eyes. 'I forgive you, yes.' He nodded reassuringly. Then, as her face broke into an ecstatic smile, he seemed to stiffen and draw away. 'However,' he added, his tone suddenly grown cold. 'I'm afraid there's something I must insist upon. . .'

Olinda held her breath, then felt her world shatter, as he continued, still in that icy tone, 'In the circumstances, it would not be suitable for us to continue to share the villa, so I must insist that you move out immediately. This very evening, to be precise. I'm sure Marilyn will help you with your packing.'

Then he was turning on his heel and walking away from her, into the drawing-room, without a backward glance.

CHAPTER NINE

So, THAT was it. The end of the story. And a bitter, ignominious end it had been.

As requested, Olinda had left the villa that evening. A taxi had arrived for her on the stroke of seven. 'I don't think there's any point in your staying on for dinner,' Guy had observed, as he carried her cases down the stairs. 'You may as well get settled into your hotel as quickly as possible.'

'Absolutely,' she had agreed, fighting to retain her stiff upper lip. 'And thanks for booking me into such a luxurious hotel. My last week on the island promises to be extremely agreeable.'

Guy had smiled wryly. 'It was the least I could do. I could scarcely allow you to move into that place where you were booked originally.'

'No. Quite.' Olinda had pulled a face, remembering the shabby, rundown shack that had met her frankly horrified gaze the day they had gone to cancel her booking. 'I don't think I would have liked that in the least.' Then, as she dared to meet his eyes for a moment, a shaft of pure pain went lancing through her. Had he any idea of how much he was hurting her?

It appeared he had not, as he held the taxi door open for her, then slammed it behind her as she climbed inside. And he didn't even wave, just turned away abruptly, back up the staircase to the veranda, as the cab headed silently off down the drive—then through the big gates and away from the villa. And out of his life, finally and forever.

Olinda manged to keep her poise intact throughout the twenty-minute journey to her hotel. And, though deathly pale, she betrayed not a tremor as the bellboy showed her to her room. But, alone at last, as she sank on to the bed and allowed the aching tears to flow freely, the pain in her heart was suddenly so loud that it seemed to fill the entire room.

Olinda spent the next couple of days in an orgy of regret and self-recrimination. The business of coming to terms with what she had done, she somehow feared, was going to prove impossible.

For it was not only that she had irrevocably alienated Guy—though that, to be sure, was unbearable enough. The very fact that she had stooped to such shameful conduct weighed heavily on her conscience. It had been out of character and against all her principles, and it was now only right, she decided masochistically, that she should be reaping the bitter, painful consequences. She deserved to have lost the man she loved.

She clenched her fists against the agony that tore through her. She had told herself she must be content with his foregiveness, and she had that forgiveness, so why this useless anguish? Because, she thought miserably, she loved him so desperately, and such love accepted no less than love in return.

And besides, she knew that his forgiveness had come from his head and not from his heart. The truth that cast its darkness, like the shadow of the gallows, over

er damned and tortured soul was the truth she had
een burning in his eyes. Despite his gesture of forgiveness, the man she loved despised and hated her.

It was a blow, too, to know that she had forfeited
forever the chance to discover the truth about Dolores.
For, although she no longer doubted that Guy was
innocent of all the terrible things she had once believed
of him—that belief was as firm and as sure now as her
love for him—she was suddenly obsessed with the need
to know the true story that lay behind the tragedy. It
was almost unbearable to realise that now she never
would.

It was on her second day at the hotel that she missed
her gold pendant, the one that had been a gift from her
mother. She had searched assiduously through her
belongings, not once but a dozen times, turning up in
the process the scrap of paper on which Elliot had
scribbled his address and phone number.

She had smiled wryly to herself as she crumpled it
up, remembering Guy's comments and how right he
had been. Elliot was not the type of man she needed.
In fact, there was only one man in the world who was.
Pain had squeezed through her, making her tremble.
How cruel that he was also one man she would never
have!

She had thrown the address away—she would never
now use it; what was Elliot now but a reminder of
Guy?—and returned her attention to the missing
locket. She had obviously left it at the villa, she
decided, her heart sinking at the thought. Had it been
anything else, she would have left it, but the pendant
had been a gift on her twenty-first birthday and, of all

her jewellery, she was particularly attached to it. Like it or not, there was only one solution. She had to contact the villa and try to get it back.

She phoned next morning, praying that Guy would not answer, and was relieved when Marilyn picked up the phone. After a brief exchange of greetings, Olinda explained her dilemma and asked Marilyn if she would mind making a very quick search. If the locket was there, then perhaps Marilyn could get it back to her, without the need for her to make a personal visit to the villa.

But such a painless solution, alas, was not to be.

'I'm sorry, there's no sign of it, miss,' Marilyn reported when, a few minutes later, she returned to the phone. 'I reckon you'd better come and look for it yourself.' Then she added quickly, correctly interpreting Olinda's hesitation, 'Mr Guy's just gone out. He said not to expect him back before lunch.'

So there was nothing else for it. She was caught in a trap. 'OK,' Olinda agreed reluctantly. 'I'll be over in about an hour.'

She hired a taxi from the hotel, her stomach in knots as she climbed inside. Then in a fit of sudden funk she requested the cab-driver to stop off for a moment at the post office first. There might be a letter from the *Bugle*, she rationalised. A confirmation of the telegram she'd sent. And besides, she was desperate for any excuse that would delay, even briefly, her return to Silver Cove.

Somewhat to her surprise, there was indeed a letter waiting for her at the *poste restante*. Resolving to read it later when she was feeling a little calmer, she stuffed it in her bag and climbed back into the taxi. Now there were no more excuses left. Like it or not, her next stop must be the villa.

The journey took a fraction of the usual time—or so, at least, it seemed to Olinda—and all too soon the cab was turning into the achingly familiar driveway that led to the villa. 'Wait,' she instructed the driver, as he parked beneath the veranda, and, heart in mouth, she began to climb out. 'I should only be a couple of minutes.'

Then she was hurrying up the wooden staircase and through the reception rooms to the bedroom, eyes fixed straight ahead, as though they were blinkered, knowing she dared not glance around her, lest the pain of her memories engulf and immobilise her.

Through in the bedroom she scanned the dressing-table where she had felt certain the pendant would be, but, as Marilyn had insisted, there was no sign of it.

Warily she opened the wardrobe door, fearing the sights and scents that would assail her. The empty hangers where her own clothes had been and the familiar male perfume that hung in the air and clung like a taunting bitter-sweet memory to the row of trousers and jackets and shirts. If she closed her eyes, he was right there beside her.

Pain like a vice wound round her heart and, impatiently, she snapped her foolish eyes open. She hadn't come here to torture herself! She had come to look for her missing pendant!

And there was no sign of it on any of the shelves that now housed neat piles of T-shirts and sweaters. She began to turn away and abort her painful mission, when, out of the corner of her eye, she caught a glint of something metallic on the floor. Relief flooded through her, as she bent to investigate. There, in a corner, lay her pendant!

Instantly she snatched it up. So this ordeal had not been in vain, after all! Then she was hurrying outside, heading for the veranda, desperate to escape.

But at the top of the staircase she suddenly paused. It would be rude to leave without speaking to Marilyn. She turned in her tracks and headed for the kitchen. 'Marilyn! Are you there?' she called.

A quick investigation, however, determined that she wasn't. She was down in the garden, hanging out some washing and chatting animatedly to the gardener. Olinda tapped on the window to attract her attention and, with her usual luminous beam of a smile, Marilyn waved back and indicated that she would only be a couple of minutes.

With a sigh, Olinda leaned against the table and urged herself to try to relax. Her mission had been successfully accomplished and there was really no reason for her to fret. It was only just after ten o'clock. Guy wouldn't be back for ages yet.

She opened her bag to deposit her pendant and was just about to pull the zipper shut when her eyes fell on the letter from the *Bugle*. She pulled it out and ripped it open. She might as well have a glance at its contents while she was waiting for Marilyn to appear.

A couple of minutes later, in stricken silence, she had read halfway through the typewritten document inside. And though her eyes kept jumping back to check that she had read correctly, her brain seemed stubbornly incapable of digesting the monstrous story

that was written there. She staggered to the front door
and paid off the taxi, then returned to the kitchen and
slumped down in a chair. For suddenly she was in no
hurry to leave. She had no intention of leaving at all.

She glanced again at her watch. It was a quarter past
ten, and Marilyn had said he would not be back before
lunch. But even if she had to wait till Doomsday, she
would not move from this house until Guy returned.

And then she would demand a full explanation of the
mind-blowing contents of the pile of pages that still
scorched like gunpowder in her hand.

Guy walked in through the front door just before one
and faltered ever so slightly in his tracks at the sight of
Olinda waiting in the hall.

'To what do I owe this unexpected pleasure?' His
tone was abrasive as he met her eyes.

But nothing, not even this display of hostility, could
have discouraged Olinda now. She had been alternately
sitting in her chair in the kitchen and pacing the hallway
for more than two and a half hours. Her grey eyes
steady, her mouth a firm line, she raised the envelope
in her hand. 'I want an explanation of this!' she
demanded, thrusting it unceremoniously at him. 'It was
sent to me by that columnist at the *Bugle* and it's all
about you. . .you and Dolores.' She took a deep breath
as her voice wavered slightly. 'I want you to tell me
that it isn't true!'

Guy did not even deign to glance at the envelope.
He regarded her with icy blue eyes. 'I see you're still in
contact with these people. I thought you told me you'd
finished with all that?'

'I have.' All at once she was trembling badly, the strain of the past couple of hours finally hitting her. 'They must have sent it before they got my telegram. It had been sitting at the post office for a couple of days.'

Guy gave her a long look, his expression slightly softening. 'And it contains information about your sister, you say?'

'Information about you and Dolores.'. Her voice dwindled to a croak. 'And I just can't believe it,' she added beseechingly.

'Give it to me. I'd better read it.' He took the envelope from her quivering fingers, then his hand was on her elbow and, gently but firmly, he was leading her through into the drawing-room. He bade her sit down, then crossed to the drinks trolley and poured a generous measure of rum. He handed it to her, as he took the armchair opposite her. 'You look as though you could use a drink.'

Never had a truer word been spoken, Olinda thought to herself, as she raised the glass to her lips. Just a moment before he had brought her in here she had feared that her legs might buckle beneath her. Even now, as the fiery liquid spread through her, warming her numbed senses back to life, she felt weak with shock and apprehension. She had to hold tightly to the chair-arm to remain upright.

Her eyes were fixed steadily on Guy's face, as he removed the pages from the envelope and, with a frown of concentration, began to read. And, as she waited anxiously for his comments, she was acutely conscious of the hammer of her heart and the dull, rhythmic thud of the blood in her veins.

After what seemed like an eternity, Guy finished reading. He glanced up at her slowly, making her heart shift. 'What prompted them to send you this?' he enquired.

Was he questioning its validity? Olinda dared to hope a little. 'There's a covering letter in there somewhere,' she explained, nodding towards the sheaf of papers in his hand. 'They say they made some checks on the story I told them and they want me to confirm that the information you've just read relates to the same Dolores.' She smiled a nervous smile. 'It doesn't, does it? They've got her mixed up with someone else.'

Guy leaned back against the cushions of his chair, his blue eyes narrowing as he met her anxious gaze. Then he sighed and ran one hand over his glossy dark hair, the lines of his face perceptibly tightening. 'I wish I could say otherwise, but I'm afraid I can't. Every word that's written here is absolutely true.'

His words hit Olinda like an avalanche. Stunned, she felt herself shrivel back into her armchair. 'But it can't be true!' she protested numbly. 'According to what it says in that document, my sister was a raving mental case!'

'Not so, *chérie*. You are too harsh.' Guy leaned forward abruptly, his expression intent. 'I was, perhaps, closer than anyone to your sister during the unfortunate events they write about here, and she remained what she had always been, a bright, extremely intelligent girl.' He paused with a sigh. 'She was however, alas, a little emotionally disturbed.'

'A little? You call that a little? According to what it says in those pages, she was in and out of mental hospitals, seeing countless doctors, countless psychiatrists.' Olinda slumped back in her chair, overcome by emotion. 'How can you sit there and call that a little?'

Without a word, Guy pulled his chair closer, so that they were almost seated side by side. Then he took her trembling hand in his and forced her to look into his eyes. 'Let me start at the beginning, when Dolores came to work for me. Let me tell you everything I know.' Then he clasped her hand more tightly, to calm her, and started to explain.

'As you know, it was shortly after her divorce that Dolores came to work at the Foundation. At the time I knew nothing about her personal circumstances. She just seemed to me like a slightly withdrawn, but competent and hard-working girl. It wasn't long before I began to realise, however, that she wasn't just withdrawn, she was deeply unhappy. When I spoke to her she told me about the break-up of her marriage—and all the other failed relationships she'd been through.'

He sighed. 'I tried to urge her to return to England. I thought she'd be better off nearer her family. But she refused. I think she was ashamed. She wanted you and her mother to believe she was a success.'

Olinda said nothing, but his words rang cruelly true. Dolores had always been considered the star of the family, adored and envied for her colourful lifestyle. Never once had she hinted that she might be having problems.

Guy took a deep breath, then, in the same regretful voice, carried on with his story. 'As time went on I began to realise that she was seriously in need of help.

She was withdrawn and listless, constantly tired, and forever, it seemed, on the verge of tears. I had a horrible premonition that she was heading for a breakdown and more or less insisted that she see a doctor. He, as it turned out, confirmed my suspicions, and referred her to a specialist in Paris.

That was when her stay in hospital occurred—though it was only a short stay, a matter of weeks, during which she underwent some therapy for depression. When she returned to Corsica, she seemed much better—but that was when a new set of problems arose. . .'

Guy shook his head sadly, remembering that time, and his eyes seemed to search deep into Olinda's, as he continued with this most harrowing part of his tale. 'It may have been because she felt grateful—it most certainly was not because I encouraged her—but around that time Dolores, unfortunately, seemed to develop an unhealthy obsession for me. She was forever following me around with those great big soulful sad eyes of hers, and though I told her straight that there could be no romance—she was a lovely girl, but she was not my type—she seemed reluctant to take my word for it.

'If she hadn't still been undergoing outpatient therapy in Paris—I used to fly her up there twice a week—I might have insisted more strenuously that she return to England, for, believe me, her obsession was a strain on me too.' He made a face, faintly self-mocking. 'Of course, I had no idea how far things had gone. I knew nothing about the stories she'd been writing to you and your mother about our supposed romance and impending marriage.'

As Olinda looked back into his eyes, she knew that every word of his story was true. At last she had the explanation that she had so longed for, but it provided a bitter, uncomfortable solace.

For the first time she spoke, her voice faint and ragged, as she asked him, with a lump in her throat, 'You mean when my mother and I came over on holiday you didn't know that we'd been told that the two of you were about to be engaged?'

'Good lord, no! I hadn't a clue! If I'd known, believe me, I'd have put you straight. Even after you left, I still didn't know. In fact, I didn't know until you told me yourself!'

The whole thing was almost too much to take in. How could she ever have suspected a truth such as this? And to think that this man whom she had once condemned as Dolores' destroyer was the one who, in reality, had tried to *save* her sister! Her emotions a jumble of sorrow and shame, Olinda listened with downcast eyes as Guy continued, 'I confess that when Dolores told me she was returning to England I didn't ask too many questions. I was relieved that she was going and I felt it would be the best thing for her. I fixed her up with a Harley Street specialist, to carry on the treatment she'd been having in Paris, and told her to keep in touch with me. She did for a while, and when the letters stopped I just assumed that she'd made a new, independent life for herself and didn't need the contact with me any more.'

He broke off as a sharp note of pain caught his voice,

then composed himself and added softly, 'When I heard that she'd died, that she'd taken her own life, I promise you I was devastated.'

At the undisguised note of self-reproach in his voice, Olinda jerked forward with concern on her face. 'But surely, after all you did for her, you don't blame yourself for that?'

He raised bitter blue eyes to look into hers. 'Perhaps a little. Yes, I do. I've often thought that if I'd told you and her mother about her breakdown and all the treatment she'd received, you might have been better able to help her, and the terrible tragedy of her death could have been prevented. The only reason I didn't say anything was that Dolores swore me to secrecy, and because I thought, perhaps mistakenly, that, as a grown woman, she had a right to her privacy.'

This time it was Olinda's turn to squeeze his hand kindly. 'Look, I loved my sister, but I know what she was like. She was an exceedingly proud and independent person, perhaps too much so for her own good. She would never have allowed Mum and me to help her. That she allowed you to help her was already a miracle—and for that I can never thank you enough.'

Her eyes misted with tears and, on a sudden impulse, she leaned forward and touched his cheek with her lips. 'No one could fault you in your treatment of Dolores. You were a good and loving friend to her.'

He smiled at that. '*Chérie, chérie. . .*'

But Olinda hadn't finished yet. Her expression earnest, she demanded to know, 'But why didn't you tell me all this before? Why didn't you tell me the other day when I threw all those ridiculous accusations at you?'

He reached out one hand to touch her hair. 'Believe me, I was tempted. But, as I told you, I promised Dolores that I would never breathe a word to her family.'

'You mean you were prepared to let me go on believing you might be guilty, just because of some silly promise?'

His fingers pushed the soft hair back from her temples, sending a delicious warm shiver over her scalp. 'It wasn't a silly promise, it was a very serious one—and I'm afraid I'm old-fashioned; I don't break promises easily.'

He tucked a stray strand of hair behind her ear and smiled a gently self-deprecating smile. 'I confess it was something of an unpleasant shock—and right on top of the shock of discovering your identity—to discover that you blamed me for your sister's death. That Dolores' family might blame me for her suicide was a possibility that had never entered my head. But, aside from not wanting to break my promise, I felt that to tell you the truth would simply upset you and, in the end, serve no useful purpose.'

Suddenly Olinda's soul was vibrant with anguish to know how cruelly she had once misjudged him—and to know too, finally, what she had so long suspected: that he was a man more than worthy of her love. She looked into his face and, in a small voice, told him, 'You'll never know how ashamed I am of what I did. If only it were possible to undo it!'

He looked into her face for a long, wordless moment,

his fingers still loosely around her hand. 'Alas, none of us can undo the past, but, as I already told you, I don't hold it against you. Besides, over the past two days I've had a chance to do some thinking, and I think I can understand why you did it. You obviously cared very much for your sister and believed she'd been done a terrible wrong. However, I'm also pretty sure,' he added quickly, arching one devil's wing eyebrow wryly, 'that the way you acted was quite out of character. I'm sure you don't normally go in for such extreme measures.'

'Absolutely not!' Olinda was quick to assure him, relieved that he had at least figured out that much about her. 'It was the first time I've ever done anything even remotely like it, and I can assure you I'll never do anything like it again.'

'I'm glad to hear it. So don't torture yourself. No real harm has been done, after all.' Guy patted her hand, then released it abruptly and started to rise up from his chair. 'Besides, none of this would have happened if I hadn't tried to force you to co-operate with me. If I hadn't twisted your arm with all my stupid threats— none of which I was serious about, incidentally—we could both have been saved a great deal of anguish.'

As he turned away, his hands thrust into his pockets, and stood looking out on to the veranda, Olinda followed him with bleak, sorrowful eyes. Her own personal anguish was almost unbearable and it would take forever, she knew, to overcome. 'Does that mean you don't hate me?' she asked in a small voice. At least knowing that would be some kind of solace.

He seemed to have to consider his answer, and the

long pause was like a cold hand closing around her heart. Then at last he said, 'No, I don't hate you. At least, not for the stories you told the newspaper. I assure you, absolutely, I've forgiven you for that.'

Olinda frowned at the broad back that was turned to her. What on earth did he mean by that? 'Do you have something else against me, then? Do you have some other reason I don't know about to hate me?'

'Not hate, *chérie*. That word is too strong—and, in the circumstances, quite inappropriate.' He paused and sighed, his shoulders lifting, then falling. 'It would be more accurate, perhaps, to say I was disappointed. Suffering from a case of badly bruised ego.' He half turned round to look at her, an expression of self-mockery in the cobalt-blue eyes. 'Don't worry, I'll get over it. It's no more than I deserve.'

Now he was really talking in riddles. Olinda leaned forward in her chair, curious and oddly apprehensive. 'Why should your ego be feeling bruised? I thought your ego,' she added, poking mild fun, 'was a more or less iron-clad commodity?'

He turned round more fully, the light on his face catching an expression of wry vulnerability. 'Then you know very little about the male ego, *chérie*. There is nothing in the world more easily deflated. For a man to discover that a woman has been faking, when he had been fool enough to believe that she cared for him a little, is, to put it bluntly, like a kick in the groin. That was why I couldn't bear to have you around. That was why I sent you away.'

He took one hand from his pocket and ran it through

his hair, shaking his head in resignation. 'But, as I said, I brought it on myself.'

All at once Olinda's heart was beating faster. On the edge of her chair, she demanded quietly, 'And why should you care if I was faking?'

Guy stuffed his hand back into his trouser pocket. 'You really want your pound of flesh!' He met her gaze with unblinking blue eyes. 'Because, unlike you, *chérie*, I wasn't.'

The words fell before her like an offering, and for one blissful, stunned moment she could not reply. Then, in a voice that was little more than a nervous croak, she answered, 'You're wrong, you know. I wasn't faking either.'

He remained very still and, all around them, time and the universe seemed suddenly suspended. Then when he spoke, his voice seemed to come from another planet. 'Surely you were simply putting on an act,' he was saying, 'so that you could get around me, and get hold of some story?'

'It started out like that.' Her mouth was as dry as cardboard. 'But I pretty soon discovered I didn't need to fake. All those feelings that I showed you——' she paused and licked her lips '—there was nothing fake about them. They were genuine. Utterly for real.'

Without seeming to move, he had come towards her, and was reaching down now to take her two hands in his. 'You really mean that?' He drew her to her feet to stand before him. 'You really mean to say that the girl I love wasn't just making a fool of me?'

What had he said? Olinda blinked at him owlishly. 'Would you mind repeating that, please?'

Instantly he obliged. 'I love you, *chérie*. I've loved your virtually from the beginning.'

'And I love you.' She could scarcely believe she'd said it. All at once, her heart was singing.

'*Chérie, chérie*. . .' His arms were about her, drawing her to him, his lips searching for hers. And all the love and the need that burned within him ignited her soul in a fierce, urgent kiss.

For, now that all the fighting and the misunderstandings were over, the loving could finally begin.

Still wrapped tightly in each other's arms, they almost floated through to the bedroom and lay down together on the big double bed. Between kisses Guy subtly discarded her clothing—the thin blue T-shirt, the flowery cotton skirt, her lacy briefs and matching bra—dropping each item carelessly to the floor, and encouraging her to do likewise with his things.

Then they twined together, two naked bodies, one soft and yielding, the other hungry and hard, exchanging whispered words of adoration as their kisses grew more breathless and their caresses more urgent, each drawing the other towards the long-postponed consummation that their bodies had ached for from the start.

And, when it came, that moment was one that Olinda would remember, and treasure, all her life. It was a moment of pleasure, of pain, of perfection. A moment as unique and intensely precious as the never-ending love they shared.

Later, as they lay curled together, their bodies warm and moist with love beneath the scented linen sheet, she felt Guy's fingers twine through her tumbled hair and draw her face gently round to look at him.

'I want you to know I don't make a habit of that,' he told her with a smile in his eyes.

Olinda frowned a little, uncomprehending. 'What don't you make a habit of?' she wanted to know.

'Making love to the various young ladies whose names appear with mine in the gossip columns.' As she started to laugh, Guy stopped her with a kiss. 'Seriously, *chérie*, I want you to believe that not a fraction of the stories you've read about me are true.'

She feigned disappointment, kissing him back. 'You mean you're not the great lover I thought you were?' she teased.

'If by great you mean good, then yes, I am.' With a playful growl, he cupped her breast in his hand and bent his head to prove his point, making her arch her back as a dart of sheer pleasure went piercing wantonly through her loins. Then he kissed his way up her throat to her mouth and paused to look earnestly into her eyes. 'But if by great you mean that I've made love to countless hundreds of women, then I'm afraid I'm not your man. I've wined and dined scores of women in my life, but I've slept with very few of them.'

With a smile she twined her arms around his neck, responding to the serious look in his eyes. 'I believe you,' she told him. And she did. And it pleased her to know that it was the truth.

Then he proceeded to take her breath away as he kissed her hair and went on to elaborate, 'And I want you to know that you're the very first I have ever proposed marriage to.'

For a fraction of a second Olinda totally forgot the desire his caresses were arousing. Her arms froze stiffly around his neck. Her breath seemed to catch and choke in her throat. 'What exactly did you say?' she croaked.

'I said I want to marry you, *chérie*. I want you to be mine for all of my life.'

She gazed into his eyes and saw the love there, and the honesty and the strength and the goodness and the passion. And for a moment the happiness that went surging through her was so intense it felt almost like pain.

As she looked into his eyes, her soul poured into his. 'Oh, yes!' she murmured. 'Oh, yes! Oh, yes!'

He drew her close to him then in a fierce embrace, as though he would never let her go, his lips kissing her eyes, her cheeks, her hair, drowning her in a sweet, warm torrent of love. 'We shall be married soon,' he promised. 'I cannot live without you now. As soon as we leave here, we shall fly to England and explain everything, gently, to your mother.' He drew back with a worried look. 'Do you think she will accept me if, like you, she believed that I was responsible for the death of Dolores?'

Olinda kissed away his frown. 'Once she knows the truth, my mother will love you as I do. On that score, I assure you, you need have no worries.'

'I want no one to love me as you do, *chérie*.' He smiled as his hand swept down across her body, caressing her breasts, the curve of her belly, the smooth, gentle roundness of her thighs. 'And no other lover to love you but me.'

He moved against her, his hardness stirring, his breath rough and ragged in his throat. 'I will be your lover till the end of your days, and I will love you and satisfy your every need.'

A shiver went through her. She pressed against him. 'Prove it!' she murmured in throaty challenge.

'I will, *chérie*,' he promised, smiling.

And he did. Over and over and over again.

HARLEQUIN

Romance

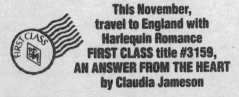

**This November,
travel to England with
Harlequin Romance
FIRST CLASS title #3159,
AN ANSWER FROM THE HEART
by Claudia Jameson**

It was unsettling enough that the company she worked for
was being taken over, but Maxine was appalled at the
prospect of having Kurt Raynor as her new boss. She was
quite content with things the way they were, even if the
arrogant, dynamic Mr. Raynor had other ideas and was
expecting her to be there whenever he whistled. However
Maxine wasn't about to hand in her notice yet; Kurt had
offered her a challenge and she was going to rise to it—after
all, he wasn't asking her to change her whole life . . . was
he?

"INDULGE A LITTLE" SWEEPSTAKES

HERE'S HOW THE SWEEPSTAKES WORKS

NO PURCHASE NECESSARY

To enter each drawing, complete the appropriate Official Entry Form or a 3" by 5" index card by hand-printing your name, address and phone number and the trip destination that the entry is being submitted for (i.e., Walt Disney World Vacation Drawing, etc.) and mailing it to: Indulge '91 Subscribers-Only Sweepstakes, P.O. Box 1397, Buffalo, New York 14269-1397.

No responsibility is assumed for lost, late or misdirected mail. Entries must be sent separately with first class postage affixed, and be received by: 9/30/91 for the Walt Disney World Vacation Drawing, 10/31/91 for the Alaskan Cruise Drawing and 11/30/91 for the Hawaiian Vacation Drawing. Sweepstakes is open to residents of the U.S. and Canada, 21 years of age or older as of 11/7/91.

For complete rules, send a self-addressed, stamped (WA residents need not affix return postage) envelope to: Indulge '91 Subscribers-Only Sweepstakes Rules, P.O. Box 4005, Blair, NE 68009.

© 1991 HARLEQUIN ENTERPRISES LTD.   DIR-RL

"INDULGE A LITTLE" SWEEPSTAKES

HERE'S HOW THE SWEEPSTAKES WORKS

NO PURCHASE NECESSARY

To enter each drawing, complete the appropriate Official Entry Form or a 3" by 5" index card by hand-printing your name, address and phone number and the trip destination that the entry is being submitted for (i.e., Walt Disney World Vacation Drawing, etc.) and mailing it to: Indulge '91 Subscribers-Only Sweepstakes, P.O. Box 1397, Buffalo, New York 14269-1397.

No responsibility is assumed for lost, late or misdirected mail. Entries must be sent separately with first class postage affixed, and be received by: 9/30/91 for the Walt Disney World Vacation Drawing, 10/31/91 for the Alaskan Cruise Drawing and 11/30/91 for the Hawaiian Vacation Drawing. Sweepstakes is open to residents of the U.S. and Canada, 21 years of age or older as of 11/7/91.

For complete rules, send a self-addressed, stamped (WA residents need not affix return postage) envelope to: Indulge '91 Subscribers-Only Sweepstakes Rules, P.O. Box 4005, Blair, NE 68009.

© 1991 HARLEQUIN ENTERPRISES LTD.   DIR-RL

INDULGE A LITTLE—WIN A LOT!

Summer of '91 Subscribers-Only Sweepstakes

OFFICIAL ENTRY FORM

This entry must be received by: Sept. 30, 1991
This month's winner will be notified by: Oct. 7, 1991
Trip must be taken between: Nov. 7, 1991—Nov. 7, 1992

YES, I want to win the Walt Disney World® vacation for two. I understand the prize includes round-trip airfare, first-class hotel and pocket money as revealed on the "wallet" scratch-off card.

Name _____

Address _____ Apt. _____

City _____

State/Prov. _____ Zip/Postal Code _____

Daytime phone number _____
                              (Area Code)

Return entries with invoice in envelope provided. Each book in this shipment has two entry coupons—and the more coupons you enter, the better your chances of winning!

© 1991 HARLEQUIN ENTERPRISES LTD.   CPS-M1

INDULGE A LITTLE—WIN A LOT!

Summer of '91 Subscribers-Only Sweepstakes

OFFICIAL ENTRY FORM

This entry must be received by: Sept. 30, 1991
This month's winner will be notified by: Oct. 7, 1991
Trip must be taken between: Nov. 7, 1991—Nov. 7, 1992

YES, I want to win the Walt Disney World® vacation for two. I understand the prize includes round-trip airfare, first-class hotel and pocket money as revealed on the "wallet" scratch-off card.

Name _____

Address _____ Apt. _____

City _____

State/Prov. _____ Zip/Postal Code _____

Daytime phone number _____
                              (Area Code)

Return entries with invoice in envelope provided. Each book in this shipment has two entry coupons—and the more coupons you enter, the better your chances of winning!

© 1991 HARLEQUIN ENTERPRISES LTD.   CPS-M1